AN AMERICAN ROBINSON CRUSOE

FOR AMERICAN BOYS AND GIRLS

SAMUEL B ALLISON

AN AMERICAN ROBINSON CRUSOE

I

ROBINSON WITH HIS PARENTS

There once lived in the city of New York, a boy by the name of Robinson Crusoe. He had a pleasant home. His father and mother were kind to him and sent him to school. They hoped that he would study hard and grow up to be a wise and useful man, but he loved rather to run idle about the street than to go to school. He was fond of playing along the River Hudson, for he there saw the great ships come and go. They were as big as houses. He watched them load and unload their cargoes and hundreds of people get off and on. His father had told him that the ships came from far distant lands, where lived many large animals and black men. His father told him too, that in these faraway countries the nuts on the trees grew to be as large as one's head and that the trees were as high as church steeples.

When Robinson saw the ships put out to sea, he would watch them till they would disappear below the horizon far out in the ocean, and think, "Oh, if I could only go with them far away to see those strange countries!" Thus he would linger along the great river and wish he might find an opportunity of making a voyage. Often it would be dark before he would get home. When he came into the house his mother would meet him and say in a gentle voice, "Why, Robinson, how late you are in getting home! You have been to the river again."

Then Robinson would hang his head and feel deeply ashamed, and when his father, who was a merchant, came home from the store, his mother would tell him that Robinson had again been truant.

This would grieve his father deeply and he would go to the boy's bedside and talk earnestly with him. "Why do you do so?" he would say. "How often have I told you to go to school every day?" This would for a time win Robinson back to school, but by the next week it had been forgotten and he would again be loitering along the river in spite of his father's remonstrances.

II

ROBINSON AS AN APPRENTICE

In this way one year after another slipped by. Robinson was not more diligent. He was now almost sixteen years old and had not learned anything. Then came his birthday. In the afternoon his father called him into his room. Robinson opened the door softly. There sat his father with a sad face. He looked up and said, "Well, Robinson, all your schoolmates have long been busy trying to learn something, so that they may be able to earn their own living. Paul will be a baker, Robert a butcher, Martin is learning to be a carpenter, Herman a tailor, Otto a blacksmith, Fritz is going to high school, because he is going to be a teacher. Now, you are still doing nothing. This will not do. From this time on I wish you to think of becoming a merchant. In the morning you will go with me to the store and begin work. If you are attentive and skillful, when the time comes you can take up my business and carry it on. But if you remain careless and continue to idle about, no one will ever want you and you must starve because you will never be able to earn a living."

So the next morning Robinson went to the store and began work. He wrapped up sugar and coffee, he weighed out rice and beans. He sold meal and salt, and when the dray wagon pulled up at the store, loaded with new goods, he sprang out quickly and helped to unload it. He carried in sacks of flour and chests of tea, and rolled in barrels of coffee and molasses. He also worked some at the desk. He looked into the account books and saw in neat writing, "Goods received" and "Goods sold." He noticed how his father wrote letters and reckoned up his accounts. He even took his pen in hand and put the addresses on the letters and packages as well as he could.

But soon he was back in his careless habits. He was no longer attentive to business. He wrapped up salt instead of sugar. He put false weights on the scales. He gave some too much and others too little. His hands, only, were in the business, his mind was far away on the ocean with the ships. When he helped unload the wagons, he would often let the chests and casks drop, so that they were broken and their contents would run out on the ground. For he was always thinking, "Where have these casks come from and how beautiful it must be there!" And many times packages came back because Robinson had written the name of the place or the country wrong. For when he was writing the address, he was always thinking, "You will be laid upon a wagon and will then go into the ship." One day he had to write a letter to a man far over the sea. He could stand it no longer. His father had gone out. He threw down the pen, picked up his hat and ran out to the Hudson to see the ships, and from that time on he spent more time loitering along the river than he did in the store.

III

ROBINSON'S DEPARTURE

Robinson's father soon noticed that his son was no longer attending to his work, and one morning sent for him to come to his office. When Robinson came in his father arose from his chair and looked him long and earnestly in the face. Then he said, "I am very sorry, Robinson, that you seem determined to continue your evil ways. If you do not do better you will grow up to be a beggar or worse." Robinson cast his eyes down and said, "I do not want to be a merchant, I would rather sail in a ship around the world." His father answered, "If you do not know anything you cannot be of use on a ship, and no one will want you. In a strange land you cannot live without working. If you run away from your parents you will come to be sorry for it." Robinson wept, for he saw that his father was right, and he promised to obey.

After two or three weeks, Robinson went to his mother and said, "Mother, won't you go to father and tell him that if he will only let me take one voyage and it proves to be unpleasant, I will come back to the store and work hard?" But the mother cried. With tears in her eyes, she said: "Robinson, your brothers are both dead. You are the only child left to us and if you go away, we shall be entirely alone. How easy it would be to be drowned in the sea, or torn to pieces by wild animals away there in a foreign country. Both your father and myself are getting along in years and who will take care of us when we are sick? Do not cause us the grief we must suffer if you go away so far amid so many dangers. I cannot bear to have you speak of it again."

Robinson did not speak of it again, but he did not forget it. He was nineteen years old. It was one day in August that Robinson stood at the wharf looking longingly after the departing ships. As he stood there, someone touched him on the shoulder. It was a ship captain's son. He pointed to a long ship and said, "My father sails to-day in that ship for Africa and takes me with him."

"Oh, if I could only go with you!" cried Robinson.

"Do come along," cried his comrade.

"But I have no money," said Robinson.

"That doesn't make any difference," returned the captain's son. "We will take you anyway."

Robinson, without thinking for a moment, gave his friend his hand and promised to go with him.

So without saying "Good-bye" to his parents, Robinson went immediately on board the ship with his friend. This happened on the 10th of August.

IV

ROBINSON FAR FROM HOME

ROBINSON'S VOYAGE

Once on board, Robinson watched the preparations for departure. At command the sailors clambered up into the rigging and loosened the sails. Then the captain from his bridge called out, "Hoist the anchor!" Then the great iron hooks that held the ship fast were lifted up, a cannon sounded a final farewell. Robinson stood on the deck. He saw the great city shimmer in the sunshine before him. Very fast now the land was being left behind. It was not long until all that could be seen of his native city was the tops of the highest towers. Then all faded from sight. Behind, in front, right and left, he saw nothing but waters.

He became a little afraid. At noon there arose a strong wind and the ship rocked to and fro. He became dizzy and had to hold fast to something. The masts and rigging began to dance. It seemed to him as if all was turning around. Suddenly he fell full length on the deck and it was impossible for him to get up. He was seasick. He wailed and cried, but no one heard him, no one helped him. Then he thought of his home, his parents whom he had so ungratefully left.

He had been on the water about two weeks when one day as he lay in his room, Robinson heard people over his head running about and crying, "A storm is coming!" The ship's sides trembled and creaked. The ship was tossed like a nutshell. Now it rolled to the right, now to the left. And Robinson was thrown from one side to the other. Every moment he expected the ship to sink. He turned pale and trembled with fear. "Ah, if I were only at home with my parents, safe on the land," he said. "If I ever get safe out of this, I will go home as quickly as I can and stay with my dear parents!" The storm raged the whole day and the whole night. But on the next morning the wind went down and the sea was calm. By evening the sky was clear and Robinson was again cheerful. He ran about the ship. He looked at the glittering stars and was contented and happy.

V

THE SHIPWRECK

Several weeks went by. Robinson had long ago forgotten his resolutions to return home. It was very hot. The glowing sun beat down upon the ship. The wide surface of the sea glistened. No breeze stirred. The sails hung loose on the top of the mast. But far away on the shore could be seen a black bank of clouds.

All at once the ship was thrown violently to one side by a fierce gust of wind. Robinson threw himself on the deck. The sea began to rise and fall. The waves were as high as mountains. Now the ship was borne aloft to the skies, and now it would seem that it must be overwhelmed in the sea. When it sank down between the great waves of water, Robinson thought it would never again rise. The waves beat violently on the ship's side. Robinson went down the steps into his little room, but he came back full of anxiety. He believed every minute he would meet death in the waves. The night at last came on. The lightning flashed. The storm howled. The ship trembled. The water roared. So the night wore on. The storm raged for six days. Then on the seventh day it was somewhat abated. But the hope was soon dashed. The storm had abated but to get new strength. Suddenly it bore down with frightful power on the doomed vessel, struck it, and shot it like an arrow through the water. Then Robinson felt a fearful crash. The ship groaned as if it would fall into a thousand pieces. It had struck a rock and there held fast. At the same moment the sailors raised the cry, "The ship has sprung a leak!" The water surged into the ship. All called for help. Each one thought only of himself. There was only one boat. The others had all been torn away. It was soon let down into the sea. All sprang in. For a moment the sailors forgot the waves, but all at once a wave, mountains high, struck the boat and swallowed it up. Robinson shut his eyes. The water roared in his ears. He sank into the sea.

VI

ROBINSON SAVED

Robinson was borne down far, far into the ocean. He attempted to work himself up, so that he could see light and breathe the air. But again and again the waves carried him down. Finally a wave threw him up and he saw, for a moment, the light of day and got a breath of air, but the next instant he was deep under the water. Then another wave bore him on its crest. He breathed a deep breath and at the same time saw land not far away. He bent all his strength toward reaching the land. He got almost to it, when a wave caught him and hurled him on a jutting rock. With all his strength he seized the rock with both hands and held on.

Presently he worked himself up a little and at last got a foothold. But, scarcely had he done so, when his strength left him and he fell on the ground as one dead. But he soon revived. He opened his eyes and looked around. He saw above him the blue sky, and under him the solid brown earth, and before him the gray angry sea. He felt to see if he still breathed. The storm had destroyed the ship. The waves had overwhelmed the boat. The water wished to draw him into the deep. The rocks seemed to want to hurl him back, but storm and wave and rock had accomplished nothing. There was One who was stronger than they.

Then Robinson sank on his knees and folded his hands. Tears came to his eyes. He breathed hard. At last he said, "Dear Father in Heaven, I live. Thou hast saved me. I thank Thee."

VII

THE FIRST NIGHT ON LAND

"Where are my companions?" That was his first thought. He began to call and halloo: "Where are you?" "Come here!" But no one answered. Then he wished to see if anyone lived on the land, and he cried, "Is there no one here? Hello!" but all remained still.

All at once he drew himself together and shrank back. He heard a bush rustle and the thought came like a flash, "That is a wild animal that will pounce upon me and tear my flesh with his teeth and claws. How shall I save myself? Where shall I fly for safety? Where shall I turn? I have nothing but my clothes and my life saved from the water. All that I had the waves have swallowed up."

And then hunger and thirst began to trouble him. He had eaten nothing the whole day and the salt water had made him sick.

In the meantime the night had come on. Robinson was very tired. Everything was new and strange. He did not know which way to move.
He was in the greatest terror.

He expected to hear the roar of wild beasts from every secluded spot. Lions and tigers and dreadful serpents filled his thoughts. He must find shelter from them. But where should he pass the night? Not a house, a hut or a cave was to be seen. He stood a long time hesitating and did not know what to do. Finally he thought, "I will do as the birds do and get into a tree." He very soon found a tree which had such thick branches that it would hold him up.

Robinson climbed up into the tree, made himself as comfortable as possible, said his prayers, and as he was thoroughly exhausted, he soon fell asleep. When he awoke the sun was high in the sky. At first he could not remember where he was. Then the truth burst upon him. He tried to move. He was stiff and sore. His flesh was bruised from being thrown against the rocks and beaten by the waves.

He was dreadfully thirsty. His mouth and throat were dry and parched from the salt water. His tongue was thick and swollen. He said, "I must find some water to drink or I shall die!"

It was hard work to get down from the tree. His limbs and back ached from sitting in the tree all night At last he slipped down and fell on the ground. He clasped his hands in prayer and thanked God for keeping him through the night.

Then he got up and tried to walk. He was so weak he could not stand.

He threw himself down on the ground and began to sob and cry, "O Lord, do not let me die! Do not let me die!" As he lay there he heard a queer sound. He listened. It sounded like water running over rocks. He tried to get to the place from which the sound came. He tried to walk. When he fell he crawled on his hands and knees. At last the sound was close by. He dragged himself up on the rocks. Yes, there was a spring of clear, cool, sparkling water bubbling up and trickling over the stones. Robinson was so thirsty he put his face into the water and drank and drank.

Then he sat down, and after a while he drank again and again.

After Robinson had satisfied his thirst and rested awhile, he felt much better. He said, "I must try to walk and see whether I can find something to eat." He found many kinds of fruits and berries all around him, but he was afraid to eat them, as they were strange to him and he feared they might be poisonous.

As he was walking along, all at once he spied a tall plant in the distance which had a familiar look. It looked like corn. He said to himself, "I wonder if it can be corn." At last he came near enough to recognize it. Yes, it was corn. It did not look exactly like the corn that he saw at home, but still he knew it would be safe to eat it. He broke off an ear and eagerly ate the kernels raw. Oh, how good it was! Robinson could not remember anything that tasted half so good.

He ate as much as he wanted and then filled his pockets with ears of corn for his supper. Then he went back to the spring to get another drink.

VIII

ROBINSON ON AN ISLAND

After his hunger and thirst were satisfied, Robinson thought he would try to find another dwelling place. "My legs are stiff and sore from sitting so uncomfortably last night, and there is so much danger of falling," he said. "I will climb yonder hill and look around and see on which side the houses are. I will find me a stick to help me on my way."

He broke a stick from a dry bush and climbed up the steep sides of the hill. After a half hour's climb he was on top. What a sight met his eyes! There were no houses, no huts to be seen, no smoke arose from the forest, no field could be seen. Nothing but trees and bush, sand and rock.

"I am then upon an island alone, without food, without shelter, without weapons! What will become of me?" he cried. "I am a prisoner. The island is my prison, the waves are the guards which will not allow me to get away. Will no ship ever come to set me free?"

He stretched his gaze out to the sea till his eyes ached, but he saw no ship.

Robinson came down and seated himself on a stone and considered what he should do. It was not yet noon, yet he feared greatly the next night. "I must find me a better bed," was his first clear thought.

IX

ROBINSON'S SHELTER

Robinson saw at a little distance what seemed to be a cleft or an opening in a huge rock. "If I could only get inside and find room to stay over night. The rock would protect me from rain, from the wind and wild animals better than a tree."

He long sought in vain for a place wide enough to allow him to get into the opening in the rock. He was about to give up, when he seized hold of a branch of a thorn tree growing on the side of the rock. He looked closer and saw that it grew out of the cleft in the rock. He saw, too, that at this point the opening was wider and that he had only to remove the tree in order to get in. "The hole shall be my dwelling," he said. "I must get the thorn tree out so that I can have room."

That was easily said. He had neither axe nor saw, nor knife nor spade. How could he do it? He had nothing but his hands. He tried to pull it out by the roots, but in vain. He wasn't strong enough.

"I must dig it out," said Robinson.

He scratched with his nails, but the earth was too hard. What should he do? He sought a stick with a fork in it and dug in the earth, but it was slow work. Then he found a clamshell. He did better with it, but it was hard work, and Robinson was not used to hard work. The sweat ran down his face and he had often to stop and rest in the shade. The sun burned so hot and the rock so reflected the heat that he was all but overcome. But he worked on. When evening came, he would sleep in the tree and next morning he would go at it again. On the third day the roots were all laid bare.

But the roots were fast in the clefts of the rock and he could not loosen it, try ever so hard. What would he not have given for an axe, or at least a knife. And yet he had never thought of their value when at home. He attempted to cut one root through with his clam-shell, but the shell crumbled and would not cut the hard wood.

He stood for a long time thinking, not knowing what next to do. He made up his mind that he must have something harder than the shell to cut with. Then he tried a stone with a sharp edge, but soon found he needed another one, however. He found one. Then he set the sharp one on the wood and struck it with the heavy one. In this way he slowly cut the roots in two.

On the fifth day there was yet left one big root, bigger than any of the others. Robinson got up early in the morning. He worked the whole day. Finally it gave a crack and it, too, was broken.

Robinson had only now to remove the loose earth inside the cleft. He found the opening could be made large and roomy. It was choked up with dirt. He dug out enough to allow him room enough to make a place to lie down. "In the future," he thought, "I will take out all the dirt and then I shall be comfortable."

It was then dark and the moon shone bright in the heavens. Robinson gathered a heap of dry grass and made himself a safe bed. But as he lay there he saw the moonbeams shining into his cave. He sprang up. "How easy," he thought, "for wild animals to creep in here upon me."

He crawled out and looked around. Not far from the cave he saw a large flat stone. With great trouble he rolled it to the opening of his cave, but before this the morning began to dawn. He went inside the shelter, seized the stone with both hands and rolled it into the opening till it almost closed it. "I have now a closed home. I can again stretch my legs. Wind and rain cannot get at me, nor wild animals."

X

ROBINSON MAKES A HAT

Refreshed and with renewed strength, Robinson awoke late the next morning, but he had a bad headache. The day before the hot tropic sun had beat down on his bare head, as he worked at his cave. He was so busy that he forgot to go into the shade from time to time in order to shield himself from the scorching sunshine. He felt a new need.

"I must make me a hat," said Robinson to himself. "But how?" He had no straw, no thread and no needle. He looked around for a long time, but found nothing. The sun mounted even higher in the heavens, and shone hotter and hotter. He went to seek shelter at last in the deep shade of a nearby tall plant.

As he stood there he examined the plant more carefully. "Out of these leaves," he said, "I might make a hat." He climbed up the short stem of the plant and saw that it had not only leaves as long as himself, but between the leaves were big bunches of long, thin fruit, as thick as three fingers and similar in shape to a cucumber.

He plucked the leaves and fruit and was about to eat some of the fruit when he heard near him a light stir as of some animal. He rolled the leaves and fruit together and hastened back to the cave.

The bananas, for that is what the fruit proved to be, were sweet and refreshing. After he had eaten enough he set immediately about making his hat. He broke off a couple of reeds. He bent one into a hoop. But the hoop would not hold without thread. Sometimes it was too large and sometimes too small. But it must fit his head. He pulled up grass and bound its ends together, but the grass stalks were not strong enough. He hunted until he found a tree whose inner bark was soft and came out in long fibres. He bound his reed with this. This, too, made the hoop soft so that it did not hurt his head.

When the hoop was ready and fitted to his head he found the banana leaves could not be used. Their veins ran straight out from the midrib. This made them easily torn, and besides, they were too large. They were not the best shape. He saw that leaves about a foot long with broad and tapering points would be best. He saw too, that if the leaves had their veins running parallel with the midrib they would be stronger. He made search and at length found leaves that seemed made for his purpose. They were thick and leathery and tapered from base to apex like a triangle.

He now proceeded with his hat-making. He would take a leaf and lay it on the ground with the base toward him. Then he laid the hoop on the base of the leaf, wrapped it around the hoop and fastened it with thorns. He did the same with the other leaves. The thorns were his pins. At last he pinned the tips of the leaves together at the top and the hat was ready. It looked just like a big cone, but it kept out the heat of the sun.

Robinson now had corn and bananas and when he was thirsty he drank a handful of water from the spring. He had been now nine days on the island. Every day he looked out on the sea until his eyes ached to see if he might discover a ship.

He could not understand why no ship came his way. "Who knows how long
I must wait here?" said he sorrowfully. Then the thought came to him:
"You will not be able to keep track of the days unless you write it down."

ROBINSON'S CALENDAR

The matter of keeping track of time puzzled Robinson very much. It was getting more difficult every day to keep it in his memory. He must write down the days as they slip by, but where and how? He had neither pen, ink, nor paper. Should he mark every day with a colored stone on the smooth side of the huge rock wall within whose clefts he had dug out his cave? But the rain would wash off the record and then he would lose all his bearings. Then he thought of the beach, but there the wind and waves would soon also erase it.

He thought a long time. "I must find something," he said to himself on which to keep a record. "I must also know when Sunday is. I must rest one day in the week. Yes, I must find something," he said, "on which to write." And finally he found it. He chose two trees standing near each other and then sought for a small sharp stone, which he could make still sharper by striking it on another. When he had got this pen ready he cut into the bark of one tree:

Shipwreck, Sunday, 10th of September, 1875.

He made seven cuts in a row for the seven days in the week. The first cut was longer than the others. This was to represent the Sunday. At sundown every day he made a new cut in the bark.

The other tree he called the month tree. On its stem he was to cut a mark every time his week tree told him a month had passed. But he must be careful, for the months were not of equal length. But he remembered that his teacher had once said in school that the months could be counted on the knuckles and hollows of the hand, in such a way that the long and short months could be found easily and he could tell in this way the number of days in each.

Robinson worked at enlarging his shelter a little every day. He was sorely at loss to find something in which to carry the dirt away from the entrance, or enough so that it would not choke up the opening. A large clam shell was all he could think of at present. He would carry the dirt to the entrance and some distance away, and then throw it. Fortunately the ground sloped away rapidly, so that he needed a kind of platform before his door.

He was careful to open the cleft at some distance above the large opening. For the air was damp and impure in the shelter. But with the opening made high above, fresh air was constantly passing into, and impure air out of, his cave. Light, too, was admitted in this way.

XII

ROBINSON MAKES A HUNTING BAG

Several days passed with Robinson's hat-making and his calendar-making and his watching the sea. Every day his corn and bananas became more distasteful to him. And he planned a longer journey about the island to see if something new to eat could be found.

But he considered that if he went a distance from his cave and found something it would really be of little use to him. "I could eat my fill," he said, "but that is all. And by the time I get back to my cave I will again be hungry. I must find something in which I can gather and carry food." He found nothing.

"The people in New York," he said, "have baskets, or pockets, or bags made of coarse cloth. Of them all, I could most easily make the net, perhaps, of vines. But the little things would fall out of the net. I will see whether I can make a net of small meshes."

But he soon saw that the vines did not give a smooth surface. He thought for a long while. In his garden at home his father had sometimes bound up the young trees with the soft inner bark of others. He wondered if he could use this. He stripped away the outer bark from the tree, which before had yielded him a fibre for his hat, and pulled off the long, smooth pieces of the inner bark. He twisted them together. Then he thought how he could weave the strands together. He looked at his shirt. A piece was torn off and unravelled. He could see the threads go up and down. He saw that some threads go from left to right (woof), others lengthwise (the warp).

From his study of the woven cloth, Robinson saw he must have a firmer thread than the strips of bark gave alone. He separated his bark into long, thin strips. These he twisted into strands or yarn by rolling between his hands, or on a smooth surface. As he twisted it he wound it on a stick. It was slow, hard work. Of all his work, the making of yarn or thread gave him the most trouble. He learned to twist it by knotting the thread around the spindle or bobbin on which he wound it and twirling this in the air. He remembered sadly the old spinning wheel we had seen at his grandmother's house.

His next care was something to hold the threads while he wove them in and out. He had never seen a loom.

After long study Robinson set two posts in the ground and these he bound with seventy-two strands horizontally under each other. Then he tied in the top at the left another thread and wove it in and out through the seventy-two threads. So he tied seventy-two vertical strands and wove them in and out. Thus he had a net three times as long as his foot and as wide as long. He tied the four corners together. He made a woven handle for it and put it on his shoulder like a sack, saying gleefully, "This shall be my hunting bag."

XIII

ROBINSON EXPLORES THE ISLAND

After Robinson made his hunting bag he was anxious to set off on his journey of exploring the island. So he arose very early next morning. "Before it is hot," thought he, "I will be quite a distance on my journey." He ate a couple of bananas, scooped up a few handfuls of water from the spring, stuck a few ears of corn in his hunting bag, took his stick in his hand and went forth. As he left his cave the thought struck him: "What if I could not find my cave again? How can I manage so that I can come back to it? I will go away in one direction and return the same way; but suppose I were to lose the way?"

Then he noticed his shadow pointing like a great finger from the sea toward the land. He could direct himself by that. He kept his shadow in front of him. He had noticed, too, that the wind always blew north of the point where the sun rose. This helped him. But sometimes the wind died down.

He had to climb over many rocks and pierce many thickets. At each step he saw a rich growth of plants, stems, leaves, flowers, but nothing to eat, no fruits, or nuts. At length he came to a tree as high as a small church steeple.

Then he thought of what his father had once said about the trees in strange countries. "Many are as tall as a church steeple and the nuts are as big as one's head." He looked again. Yes, there they hung among the leaves, concealed high above in the crown! But *so* high, it was well that Robinson had learned to climb while on board the ship. He quickly laid down his hunting bag and clambered up the smooth stem of the high tree, a palm. He picked off a nut and threw it down and then several more, and climbed down again.

But the nuts were very hard. How should he open them? He had brought along his sharp stone with which he had stripped off the inner bark. With this he forced off the thick outer shell. But now came the hard nut within, and how hard it was! Striking it was of no use.

Then he threw a great stone on the nut. The shell was crushed and a snow-white kernel lay before him. It tasted like almond. With astonishment Robinson saw in the middle of the nut a large empty space which must have been filled with fluid as the inside was wet. He wished that he had the juice to drink, for he was very thirsty. With this in view, he examined another and riper nut, and the outside came off more easily. But how could he break it and at the same time save the juice? He studied the hull of the cocoanut on all sides. At the ends were three little hollows. He attempted first to bore in with his fingers, but he could not. "Hold!" he cried. "Maybe I can cut them there with the point of my stone knife." This was done without trouble and out of the hole flowed the sweet, white juice.

Robinson put a couple of nuts in his hunting bag, and also the shells from the broken nuts. "Now," he thought, "I shall no longer have to drink from my hand." With this thought he went on his way.

As Robinson came to a rock in his path, out jumped what Robinson took to be a rabbit. He ran after him to catch him, but the rabbit was much the swifter. So Robinson hastened home, but before he reached it the stars were shining with their lustrous light. Tired Robinson stretched his limbs on his bed of grass and leaves and slept soundly.

XIV

ROBINSON AS A HUNTER

All the time Robinson was confined to the cave he kept thinking about the rabbit he had seen and how he might catch one. Finally, he determined to make a spear. He broke down a thin, young sapling, stripped off its branches and in one end fastened a sharp stone. He then went to bed, for he wanted to be up early for his first hunting trip on the morrow.

With his hunting sack and spear, Robinson began to creep very, very cautiously through the underbrush. But he did not go far before he saw a lot of rabbits feeding peacefully on the soft leaves and grass. He drew back and threw his spear with all his might. But the spear did not reach the rabbits. It fell far short and the rabbits sprang up and ran quickly away. He tried it several times with the same result. Then Robinson, discouraged, turned back home and ate his corn, bananas, and cocoanuts without meat. In the meantime he found a new kind of food. He discovered a nest of eggs. How good they tasted to him!

But his longing for meat was still very great. "I will try to make a bow and arrow," he said. No sooner said than done. He bent a long piece of tough, young wood and stretched between the ends a cord twisted out of the fiber taken from the cocoanut shell. He then sought for a piece of wood for arrows. He split the ends with his flint knife and fastened in splinters of stone. At the other end he fastened on some feathers found on the ground. The arrows flew through the air with great swiftness. "They will go far enough," thought Robinson, "if I could only hit anything."

He practised shooting. He stuck his stone knife in a tree and shot at it the whole day long. At first he could not hit it at all. The arrows flew far from the mark. After a while he could hit the tree, but not the knife. Then as he practised, his arm grew ever surer, until at last he could hit the knife at almost every attempt. After a few days he again went rabbit hunting. He thought that the rabbit did not offer a mark so high as his knife, so he stuck a stone in the ground and practised shooting at that. He gradually increased the distance until he could hit the mark at twenty or thirty yards.

The next morning Robinson took his bow and arrows and went out to hunt. He aimed at a rabbit, shot, and it fell, pierced by the arrow. His very first shot was successful.

He hastened up and took the dead rabbit on his shoulder, carried it to his cave and skinned it. Then he cut off a nice, large piece of meat and was going to roast it, but alas, he had no fire!

XV

ROBINSON'S SHOES AND PARASOL

The next morning Robinson could not get up. His feet were swollen and sore in consequence of walking without shoes over thorns and stones. He must remain the whole day in his cave.

Before him, in the sun, his walking stick stuck in the ground. He thought how he had been troubled yesterday to find his way and about the shadow. He had now time to study it. He watched it the whole day through. In the morning it pointed toward the land. In the evening toward the sea. This comes from the daily movement of the sun. He determined to study the matter more carefully.

Robinson got up and with great effort walked to the spring. There he cooled his burning feet, and gathered some large leaves, which he bound on them. He decided to remain in his cave a few days, for he had enough food stored up to last him some length of time. He planned how he might make himself a pair of shoes. As soon as his feet were well, he sought out some thick bark and put fastenings of tough, strong fiber on it. These served very well to protect his feet.

But he must have some further protection from the sun. It beamed so hot that his hat was not enough. He made a parasol out of leaves like his hat. He took a straight stick for a handle. He tied some reeds together and bent them into a hoop. He then fastened the upper end of the stick in the center of the hoop by means of six reeds which formed the ribs of the parasol. To keep out the sun he covered this framework with large, broad leaves. With a cord he tied the stem ends of the leaves to the stick just above where the reeds were tied.

Spread out, these broad leaves completely covered the ribs. Their tips reached over the hoop. They were fastened together by means of small, needle-like fish-bones Robinson had found on the beach.

XVI

GETTING FIRE

Now Robinson had heard that savages take two dry pieces of wood and rub them so long on each other that they at length begin to burn.

He tried it. The sweat ran down his cheeks, but every time the wood was about to catch fire his strength would give out, and he was obliged to rest, and when he began again the wood was cold.

"How will it be in winter," he cried, "when it is cold, and I have no fire?" He must try other ways of preparing meat for his table. He must think of some other way of getting fire. He remembered that once, when a boy at home, he had in playing with a stick made it hot by twirling it on end on a piece of wood. "I will try this," he thought. He searched for a good hard stick and a piece of wood upon which to turn or twirl it with his hands. Having found the best materials at hand, he began to twirl the stick. He made a little hollow in the block of wood in which to turn his upright stick. There was heat but no fire. He twirled and twirled, but he could not get the wood hot enough to blaze up or ignite. He had not skill. Besides his hands were not used to such rough treatment. Soon they blistered and this method had to be given up.

"I must have fire," he still thought, and recalled the sparks that flew from the stone pavements of the streets when the iron shoes of the horses struck them as they slipped and strained at their cruel loads. Why may I not get fire by striking together two stones? He sought out two hard stones and with great diligence kept striking them together until his strength gave out, and he was obliged again to acknowledge failure.

He remembered that sometimes travelers put the meat underneath the saddle and ride on it until it is soft. He tried it with pounding. He laid some of the meat on a flat stone and pounded it. It became quite soft and tasted very well. He then tried hanging it in the sun and finally wrapped it in leaves and buried it for a few hours in the hot sand.

XVII

ROBINSON MAKES SOME FURNITURE

One thing troubled Robinson very much. He could not sit comfortably while eating. He had neither chair nor table. He wished to make them, but that was a big job. He had no saw, no hammer, no auger and no nails. Robinson could not, therefore, make a table of wood.

Not far from his cave he had seen a smooth, flat stone. "Ay," thought he, "perhaps I can make me a table out of stone." He picked out the best stone and built up four columns as high as a table and on these he laid his large, flat stone. It looked like a table, sure enough, but there were rough places and hollows in it. He wanted it smooth. He took clay and filled up the holes and smoothed it off. When the clay dried, the surface was smooth and hard. Robinson covered it with leaves and decked it with flowers till it was quite beautiful.

When the table was done, Robinson began on a chair, He made it also of stone. It had no back. It looked like a bench. It was uncomfortable to sit on. Robinson covered it with moss. Then it was an easy seat.

Table and chair were now ready. Robinson could not move them from one corner to another, nor when he sat on the chair could he put his feet under the table, and yet he thought them excellent pieces of furniture.

Every day Robinson went hunting and shot a rabbit, but the meat would not keep. At home they would have put it in the cellar. If only he had a cellar! He saw near his cave a hole in the rock. He dug it out a little with his mussel shell and found that it led back under a rock.

From much bending over in digging, Robinson's back, unused to severe toil, ached wretchedly. He decided to make a spade. With his flint he bored four holes in a great, round mussel shell. They formed a rectangle as long as a little finger and as wide. Through these holes he drew cocoanut fibre and bound the shell to a handle fast and strong.

With his spade he dug a hole so deep that he could stand in it upright. Then he put in a couple of shelves made of flat stones. In this cellar he put his rabbit meat and his eggs. Then he laid branches over it and finally covered the whole with leaves.

XVIII

ROBINSON BECOMES A SHEPHERD

With his bow and arrow, Robinson went hunting every day. The rabbits soon learned to know him and let themselves be seldom seen. As soon as they saw him, they took alarm. They became timid and shy. One day Robinson went out as usual to shoot rabbits. He found none. But as he came to a great rock he heard from behind a new sound, one he had not heard before in the island. Ba-a-a, it sounded.

"A kid," thought Robinson, "like that with which I have so often played at home."

He slipped noiselessly around the rock and behold, really there stood a kid. He tried to call it, but the kid sought safety in flight. He hastened after it. Then he noticed that it was lame in one fore foot. It ran into some brush, where Robinson seized it by the horns and held it fast.

How Robinson rejoiced! He stroked it and fondled it. Then he thought, how could it come into this wilderness on this lonesome island? "Has your ship been cast upon the rocks too, and been broken to pieces? You dear thing, you shall be my comrade." He seized the goat by the legs, and no matter how it kicked, carried it to his cave.

Then he fetched quickly a cocoanut shell full of water and washed and bathed the goat's wounded leg. A stone had rolled down from the hill and had inflicted a severe wound on its left fore leg, or perhaps it had stepped into a crack in the rocks. Robinson tore off a piece of linen from his shirt, dipped it in water and bound it with shreds of the cocoanut upon the wound. Then he pulled some grass and moss and made a soft bed near the door of the cave. After he had given it water, it looked at him with thankful eyes and licked his hand.

Robinson could not sleep that night. He thought continually of his goat and got up time and again to see if it was safe. The moon shone clear in the heavens. As Robinson sat before the goat's bed he looked down on his new possession as lovingly as a mother on her child.

The next morning Robinson's first thought was, "I am no longer alone. I have a companion, my goat." He sprang up and looked for it. There she lay on her side, still sleeping.

As he stood and considered, the thought came to him that perhaps the goat had escaped from its keeper. There must then be some one living on the land. He quickly put on his shoes and his hat, took his parasol, and ran to the rock where he had found the goat.

He called, he sought, he peered about to see if some shepherd were there somewhere. He found nothing. He found no trace of man. There was no road, no bridge, no field, no logs, not even a chip or shaving to show that the hand of man had been there.

But what was that? In the distance ran a herd of goats over the rocks. But no dog followed them and no shepherd. They ran wild on the island. They had perhaps been left there by some ship. As he came home he noticed the goat sorrowfully. The bandage had become dry. The goat might be suffering pain. Robinson loosened the bandage, washed the wound again and bound it up anew. It was so trustful. It ran after him and he decided always to protect it.

"I will always be your shepherd and take care of you," he said.

XIX

ROBINSON BUILDS A HOME FOR HIS GOAT

But the goat was a new care. Wild animals could come and kill and carry Robinson's goat away while he slept, and if the goat got frightened while he was hunting it would run away.

"I will have to make me a little yard in front of my cave," he said, "for my goat to live in." But from whence must come the tools? He had neither hatchet nor saw. Where then were the stakes to come from? He went in search of something. After hunting for a long time he came upon a kind of thistle about two feet higher than himself, having at its top a red torch-like blossom. There were a great many of them.

"Good!" thought Robinson. "If I could only dig up enough of them and plant them thick around the door of my cave, I would have just the thing. No one could get at me, nor at the goat, either, The thorns would keep anything from creeping through, peeping in or getting over."

So he took his mussel-shell spade and went to work. It was pretty hard, but at length he succeeded in laying bare the roots of quite a number. But he could not drag them to his cave on account of the thorns sticking in him. He thought a long time. Finally, he sought out two strong poles or branches which were turned up a little at one end and like a sled runner. To these he tied twelve cross-pieces with bark. To the foremost he tied a strong rope made from cocoa fiber. He then had something that looked much like a sled on which to draw his thistle-like brush to his cave. But for one day he had done enough. The transplanting of the thistles was hard work. His spade broke and he had to make a new one. In the afternoon he broke his spade again. And as he made his third one, he made up his mind that it was no use trying to dig with such a weak tool in the hard ground. It would only break again.

"If I only had a pick." But he had none. He found a thick, hard, sharp stone. With it he picked up the hard earth, but had to bend almost double in using it. "At home," he thought, "they have handles to picks." The handle was put through a hole in the iron. He turned the matter over and over in his mind, how he might put a hole through the stone. But he found no means. He searched out a branch with a crotch at one end. He tied the stone to this with strong cocoa fiber and bark.

How his eye glistened as he looked at the new tool! Now he began to work. He first loosened up the earth with his pick, then he dug it out with his spade and planted in a high thistle. Many days he had to work, but finally one evening the hedge was ready. He had a row in a semicircle in front of his cave. He counted the marks on his calendar tree. The day on which he had begun to make his hedge he had especially marked out. He had worked fourteen days.

He had completed his hedge with the exception of a small hole that must serve for a door. But the door must not be seen from without.

As Robinson thought, it came to him that there was still place for two thistles on the outside. He could easily get in, but the entrance was difficult to find from the outside.

Robinson looked on his hedge from without. It was not yet thick enough. For this reason he planted small thistles between the larger ones. With the digging them out and transplanting them he was a whole week longer.

Finally, the hedge and the yard were ready. Now Robinson could rest without fear and sleep in his cave, and could have his goat near him all the time. It delighted him greatly. It ran after him continually like a dog. When he came back from an absence, it bleated for joy and ran to meet him as soon as he got inside the hedge. Robinson felt that he was not entirely alone. He had now a living being near him.

XX

ROBINSON GETS READY FOR WINTER

There was one thing that troubled Robinson greatly. "What will become of me when the winter comes? I will have no fire to warm me. I have no clothing to protect me from the cold, and where shall I find food when snow and ice cover all the ground and when the trees are bare and the spring is frozen? It will be cold then in my cave; what shall I do? It is cold and rainy already. I believe this is harvest time and winter will soon be here. Winter and no stove, no winter clothing, no winter store of food and no winter dwelling. What shall I do?"

He considered again the project of making fire. He again sought out two pieces of wood and sat down and rubbed them together. The sweat rolled down his face. When the wood began to get warm, his hand would become tired, and he would have to stop. When he began again the wood was cold. He worked for an hour or two, then he laid the wood aside and said, "I don't believe I can do it I must do the next best thing. I can at least get warm clothing to protect me from the rain and snow." He looked down at his worn, thin clothing, his trousers, his shirt, his jacket; they had become so thin and worn that they were threadbare.

"I will take the skins of the hares which I have shot and will make me something," he thought. He washed and cleaned them, but he needed a knife and he set about making one. He split one end of a tough piece of wood, thrust his stone blade in it and wound it with cocoa fibre. His stone knife now had a handle. He could now cut the skins quite well. But what should he do for needle and thread? Maybe the vines would do. "But they are hardly strong enough," he thought. He pulled the sinews from the bones of the rabbit and found them hard. Maybe he could use them. He found fish skeletons on the seashore and bored a hole in the end of the small, sharp rib bones. Then he threaded his bone needle with the rabbit sinews and attempted to sew, but it would not go. His needle broke. The skin was too hard. He bored holes in the edge of the pieces of skin and sewed through the holes. This went very well.

He sewed the skins together with the hair side inward, made himself a jacket, a pair of trousers, a hat, and finally covered his parasol with rabbit skin, for the rain had already dripped through the leaves of it. All went well, only the trousers did not fit. He loosened them and puckered them to no purpose. "Anyway," he thought, "I am now well protected from the cold, when it does come."

XXI

HOW ROBINSON LAYS UP A STORE OF FOOD

Now for the food. Could Robinson preserve the meat? He had often heard his mother tell about preserving meat in salt. He had even eaten salt meat, pickled meat. But where could he get salt?

One day when the wind blew hard the water was driven upon the shore and filled a little hollow. After a few days the ground glistened white as snow where the water had been. Was it snow? Robinson took it in his hands and put it in his mouth. It was salt. The sun had evaporated the water in the hollow — had vaporized it — and the air had drunk it up. What was left behind? Salt. Now he could get salt as long as he needed it.

He took cocoanut shells and strewed salt in them. Then he cut the rabbit meat in thin strips, rubbed them with salt, and laid them one on the other in the salt in the shells. He covered it over with a layer of salt. He put over each shell the half of a larger one and weighted it down with stones. After a period of fourteen days he found the meat quite red. It had pickled.

But he did not stop here. He gathered and stored in his cellar cocoanuts and corn in such quantities that he would be supplied for a whole winter. It seemed best to catch a number of rabbits, build a house for them and keep them. Then he could kill one occasionally and have fresh meat. Then it came to him that goats would be much better, for they would give milk. He determined immediately to have a herd of goats. He made a string or lasso out of cocoa fibre.

Then he went out, slipped up quietly to a herd of goats and threw the lasso over one. But the lasso slipped from the horns and the goat ran away. The next day he had better luck. He threw the lasso, drew it tight and the goat was captured. He brought it home. He rejoiced when he saw that it gave milk. He was happy when he got his first cocoanut shell full of sweet rich milk. His goat herd grew. He soon had five goats. He had no more room in his yard. He could not provide food enough. He must let them out. He must make another hedge around his yard so that the goats could get food and yet be kept from going away. He got stakes from the woods and gathered them before his cave. He sharpened them and began to drive them in the earth. But it rained more and more each day. He was wet through as he worked. He had finally to stop work, for the rain was too heavy.

XXII

ROBINSON'S DIARY

Robinson was much disturbed because he had no means of keeping a record of things as they happened from day to day. He had his calendar, it is true. He would not lose track of the time. But he wished for some way to write down his thoughts and what happened. So he kept up keen search for anything that would serve him for this purpose.

Every time he journeyed about the island he kept careful watch for something that he might write upon. He thought of the leaves of the palm tree, the white under surface of the shelf fungus. But these he found would not do. He tried many kinds of bark and leaves. There was a kind of tall reed or grass growing in the marshes whose rind seemed good when dried. He examined the inner bark of many trees. He at last found that the inner bark of a tree which resembled our elm tree worked best. He would cut through the bark with his stone knife around the tree. At about one foot from this he would cut another ring. He then would cut through the bark lengthwise from one circular cut to the other. He could then peel off the section easily. While it was yet full of sap he would separate the soft, tough, thin inner layer of the bark. This usually came off in sheets without a break. When these sheets of bark were stretched and dried they could be used very nicely instead of paper.

Robinson next searched for something that would serve him as ink, and this was much easier to find than paper. He had noticed many kinds of galls of many different colors growing on trees. He did not know what they were, or how they grew, but he had learned in his father's store that ink was often made from galls gathered from trees. "Anyway," he thought, "I can get ink from the cuttle-fish." He had watched this animal get away from its enemies by sending out a cloud of purplish fluid, in which to hide as it darted away. He had learned also that indigo is made from the leaves of a plant. He had noticed a plant growing in the open places in the forest whose leaves turned black when dried.

Robinson gathered a quantity of gall-nuts and soaked them in water. To the black fluid thus obtained he added a little rice water to make it flow well, and this served very well as an ink. He kept his ink in a cup made from a cocoanut shell.

He was not long in getting a pen, though the lack of a good sharp knife made it hard to make a good one. In going about he had gathered a quantity of large feathers. He saved these for the time when he should have his paper and ink ready. Now, he cut away a quill to a point and split it up a little way. He was now supplied with writing materials. "Is it not wonderful," he thought, "how all our wants are filled? We have only to want a thing badly enough and it comes."

Robinson began at once to write down the date for each day and the main thing he did or that happened on it. He called this his diary. He had now a better way of keeping time than on his tree calendar. He did not need it any more.

You have no doubt wondered how Robinson could work in his cave, especially at night without a light. The truth is, it was a great source of discomfort to him. At sunset he was in total darkness in his cave. During the day light enough streamed in from the open doorway. To be alone in total darkness is not pleasant. "If I only had fire!" he said again and again.

He watched the many large beetles and fireflies flash their light in the dark of the evening as he sat in front of his shelter. The thought came to him that if he only had some way of keeping together a number of them, they would serve very well for a candle in his cave at night. How he longed for a glass bottle such as he had so often wantonly broken when at home! Back of his shelter there was a hill where the rock layers jutted out. He had noticed here several times the thin transparent rock that he had seen in his father's store. It is called isinglass.

"I will make a living lantern," he said aloud in his eagerness.

He soon had a suitable piece pried loose. He cut a part of a cocoanut shell away and in its place he put a sheet of isinglass. That evening at dark he gathered several handfuls of the great fire beetles and put them in his lantern. What joy their glow gave him in his cave at night. It was almost as much comfort as a companion. But while it lighted up the deep dark of the cave and enabled him to move about, he was unable after all to write in his diary at night. Every morning he set his captives free. In the evening he would go out and capture his light.

XXIII

ROBINSON IS SICK

One evening Robinson went to bed sound and well. The next morning he was sick. Before he had only the heat of the day to complain of. To-day he was freezing. He wanted to go to work to get warm, but even this did not break his chill. It increased till his teeth chattered with the cold.

"Perhaps," thought he, "if I can sleep a little I will get better." But he could not sleep. He was burning with fever and then shaking with cold by turns. He felt a strong thirst, but he was so weak that he could scarcely get the goat's milk. He had no sooner drunk the milk than his tongue was as dry as before. He felt better after a night of sleep, but the next day his fever and chills were worse than before. Then he bethought him of his parents. How kindly his mother had taken care of him! Now no one was near that could assist him.

"Ah," he sighed, "must I die here? Who would bury me? There is no one to miss me." At this the tears came to his eyes.

His sickness increased with each day. Occasionally the fever would go down sufficiently to allow him to get something to eat. Then it would be worse than before. In his dire need he wanted to pray, but he was so weak that he could only stammer, "Dear God, help me, or I shall die!"

One night he had a strange dream. He thought he saw his good old father standing before him calling to him. He spread out his arms and cried aloud, "Here I am, here I am!" He tried to get up, but he was so weak that he fell back fainting.

He lay there a long time, but finally came to. He felt a burning thirst, but no one reached him a drop of water. He prepared to die. He folded his hands and prayed to God that he would be merciful to him. He prayed forgiveness from his parents. Once more he raised his head and gazed wildly around, then he sank back and knew no more.

When he again awoke he felt better. His hot fever had gone. He attempted to walk. He had just enough strength to crawl to the table and fetch a shell of water. When he tried to walk he had to sit down at every two or three steps.

From this he recovered gradually, growing better and better, and he thanked God inwardly for his recovery. His sickness had continued from June 18 to July 3.

ROBINSON'S BOWER

Robinson's sickness set him thinking about his home. He had been so afraid of animals when he came to the island that he thought of nothing but protection from them. He had been now a year on the island and had seen nothing more dangerous than a goat. The fear of animals had practically faded away. In thinking over his sickness he made up his mind that it was caused by sleeping in his cave where the sun never shone. The ventilation seemed good, but the walls were damp, especially in the rainy season. Then the water would trickle down through the cleft in spite of all he could do.

He resolved to build, if possible, a little cottage, or, as he called it, a bower, in the yard in front of his shelter. The hedge of thistles was growing and formed a fence that an animal could not get through. His screen of willows on the outside of this would soon hide him from view from the sea. He had the wall of rock and the hill behind him.

He planned out his way of building it very carefully. "It must be done," he said (Robinson formed the habit of talking to himself, so that he would not forget how to talk), "without hammer, nails, or saw."

He first sought out four posts, as large as he could well handle. There were always broken trees and branches in the forest. If he searched long enough he could find posts just suited to his need. He wanted four of the same thickness and height and with a fork at the end. After long searching he found what he wanted. He was careful to get those that he could drag to his shelter.

He placed these in the ground, forming the corners of a square about ten feet long. In the forks he placed poles running around about eight feet from the ground. At about every three feet he fastened others, running in the same way, with heavy cords made of fibre. He found his greatest trouble with the roof. It must be sloped to shed rain. He had to find two more forked posts, three or four feet longer than the others. These he placed opposite each other in the centers of two sides. Upon these he placed a ridge pole. He then laid other poles lengthwise from ridge pole to the edge of the frames.

His frame was now done. His plan was now to cover this frame with straw or grasses tied in bundles. He had seen the barns in the country thatched in this way by the Dutch farmers in New York State. He gathered the straw of the wild rice. It was long, straight and tough.

It was easily tied into flat bundles. These he bound securely on to the frame work with cords. He began at the bottom so that the ends of the row would lap over the tops of the last one put on.

In this way he built a very comfortable and rainproof bower. It was easy to make a bed of poles covered with straw. A table and bench were added and shelves of poles.

Robinson felt great joy over this new home. "I will not now be sick any more," he said. "In case of danger I can get into my cave. But at all other times I will live in my bower." He had use still for his cave. He could use it to store some things in. But he had to be careful about the dampness in wet weather.

Robinson was getting to feel at home. He was no longer so sad. He did not grieve so much for home. He looked upon his home with great delight It was secure. He had his herd of goats always in his sight. At evening he would do his milking. He found he could keep the milk for some time in the cave. He was tempted to try making some butter from the good, rich cream. "But," said Robinson, "I have neither vessels to make it in nor bread to eat it on."

He planned many things to do. "I will make a hammock some day for my bower and some vessels to use in my work," he thought.

ROBINSON AGAIN EXPLORES HIS ISLAND

When Robinson recovered his strength he had a strong desire to see more of the island. At first he had been in constant fear of wild animals, but now he thought he would like to see all there was to see in the island. On the 15th of July he started out. First he went to a brook which ran into the sea near his cave. Its water was clear and pure; along its shore lay beautiful meadows. As he came to the upper course of the brook the meadow gave way to forest. On the border of the forest he found melons and grapes.

The night came on and he slept again in a tree. The next morning he went farther and came to a clear rivulet. Here the region was wonderfully beautiful. The flowers bloomed as in a garden, and near the flowers stood splendid apple and orange trees. He took as much of the fruit as he could carry and went on his way. This journey continued three days. The grapes which he had carried he dried in the sun and made raisins.

The 10th of September came, one year had passed on the island. He was many hundred miles from home, alone on an island. With tears he cried out, "Ah! what are my dear parents saying? They have no doubt long given me up as dead. If I could only send them a message to comfort them and let them know how much I love them!"

The day was celebrated as a holiday. He thanked God that He had given him so many good things. Often he had lived the whole day in care and anxiety. Now he tried to be more cheerful and to meet the troubles of each day with courage.

But Robinson was not yet satisfied. He longed to know more of the island and prepared himself for a greater journey. He slung his hunting pouch over his shoulder, filled it full of food, took his bow and arrows, stuck his stone hatchet in his belt and started on his way. He traveled over meadows, through beautiful forests in which were hundreds of birds. He was delighted as they sang and fluttered about.

The journey was beautiful and pleasant to Robinson. In the forests he often saw small wild creatures, but he shot nothing. After the first night he slept under a tree in the soft grass, for he had now no fear of wild animals.

Along the shore he saw great groves of palms with their large nuts. He saw, too, many goats in all parts of the island.

Now he was ready to take the shortest way home. He had not gone far before he came into a dark forest. He became confused and wandered about for several days. On the fourth day he came to a little pile of stones, which he had made to mark the way as he was going out. From this place the way was easy to find. On this trip he was gone already two weeks.

XXVI

ROBINSON AND HIS BIRDS

Of all the things he saw on his journey Robinson was most delighted with the birds. They were of the most beautiful colors. The forest was full of them. They gleamed like jewels in the deep masses of foliage. In the morning their singing filled the air with sound.

Robinson had never taken much notice of the birds at home. But now every living thing attracted him. He loved to see them happy. He would watch often by the hour and learn the habits of nesting and getting food of nearly every bird on the island.

Robinson did not know the names of many of the birds he saw on the island. He had to make names for them. The strangest thing he saw on his journey was the nest of what he called the yellow-tail. This bird lives in colonies and makes its nest at the ends of the long leaves of the mountain palm. When he first saw these queer looking sacks hanging from the leaves he was amazed. He had never seen so strange a sight. From the end of each great leaf hung a long, closely woven nest. Robinson could not make out at first what they were. Soon, however, he saw the birds come out of the mouths of the nests. Here, one hundred feet from the ground, they hung their nests. But they were perfectly safe.

He had not gone far from the tree in which the yellow tails had their nests when he was suddenly startled by a voice crying, "Who, who are you?" Robinson was greatly frightened and hid beneath the drooping branches of a cedar tree. He feared every moment that the owner of the voice would make his appearance. But it kept at a distance. Every few minutes from the depths of the forest would come the doleful cry, "Who, who are you?" Robinson did not dare to stir from his hiding place. He remained there over night. After the night came on he heard the strange voice no more.

The next day he renewed his journey. He saw many birds that were wholly strange to him. There was a kind of wild pigeon that built its home in a hole in the rock. It was a most beautiful bird with long, slender, graceful feathers in its tail. He saw the frigate bird soaring high above the island. The number and beauty of the hummingbirds amazed Robinson. They were of all colors. One had a bill in the shape of a sickle. The most brilliant of them all was the ruby-crested hummingbird.

Near noon, while Robinson was shielding himself from the scorching heat of the sun in a deep, shaded glen, he was startled again by the strange voice crying, "Who, who, who are you?" He lay quite still, determined if possible to allow the voice to come, if it would, within sight. He heard it slowly coming up the glen. Each time it repeated the cry it sounded nearer. At last he saw spying at him through the boughs of the tree under which he was lying a large bird with soft, silky feathers of green and chestnut. "Who, who, who are you?" said the bird. Robinson could not help but laugh. He had been frightened at the cry of a bird.

But the bird that interested Robinson most was the parrot. There were several kinds of them. They flew among the trees with great noise and clatter and shrieking. Robinson determined if possible to secure one for a pet. "I can teach it to talk," he said, "and I will have something to talk to.'" As soon as he returned home he set about catching one. He noticed that a number were in the habit of visiting an old tree near the shelter every morning. He planned to snare one and tried several mornings, but he could not get one into the snare. He tried to hit one with his bow and arrow. He at last succeeded in hitting one and stunning it so that it fell to the ground. He ran rapidly to pick it up, but before he could get to where it lay in the bushes it had disappeared.

After thinking the matter over he concluded that it would be much better to get a pair of young birds and raise them. The old ones would be hard to tame and difficult to teach. It was easy enough to find a nest in a hollow tree. He secured from the nest two birds just ready to fly. He made a cage for them out of willow rods. He placed the cage at the entrance of his cave and studied how he would feed them. Much to his surprise the parent birds discovered their young ones and brought them food and fed them through the open work of the cage.

When the birds were grown they rapidly learned to talk. Robinson took great delight in teaching them. He taught them to call his name and when he came near they would call out, "Poor old Robinson Crusoe!"

These birds remained for many years with Robinson. In fact, he was never afterward without a parrot. They helped him to pass away very pleasantly many hours that without them would have been sad.

Another bird that Robinson loved was the little house wren. This bird was exceedingly tame and friendly. It was a very sweet and strong singer. It loved to make its nest in or near his shelter. There it would build and rear its young, within reach of his hands, while its throat was always bursting with melody.

The mocking bird, too, always nested near and awakened him in the morning with its wonderful song.

Robinson became a great friend and favorite of the bird inhabitants of the island. They seemed to know him and showed no fear when near him. This pleased him very much.

XXVII

ROBINSON GETS FIRE

Robinson was now pretty comfortable. He had his bower with its chair and table. He had his cave in case of danger. He had his cellar in which to keep his meat. He would sit in the shade near the door of his bower and think of the many things he should be thankful for. But there was one hardship that Robinson could not get used to and that was the eating of raw food. "How fine it would be if only I could parch a few grains of corn in the fire! I could like live a prince," thought he, "if I had fire. I would grind some of my corn into flour and make some corn bread or cakes and cook rice." He did so long for roasted meat and determined again to make the attempt to get fire.

Robinson was fast losing his idle, thoughtless ways of doing things. He had become a thoughtful and diligent man in the short time that he had been on the island. Trouble and hardship had made a man of him. "I must carefully think over the whole matter of getting fire," he said. He had failed twice and was now resolved to succeed. "If the lightning would only strike a tree," he thought, "and set it on fire."

But he could not wait for such a thing to happen, and how could he keep it when once thus obtained? It was clear he must have some way of producing fire when he wanted it, just as they did at home? He thought over the ways he had tried and the one most likely to be successful. He resolved to make a further trial of the method by twirling a stick in his hands. He selected new wood that was hard and dry. He carefully sharpened a stick about eighteen inches long and, standing it upright in a hollow in the block of wood, began to roll it between his hands. By the time Robinson's hands were well hardened, it seemed that he was going to succeed at last. But he lacked the skill to be obtained only by long practice.

"If I could only make it go faster," he said. "There must be some way of doing this. I believe I can do it. I used to make my top spin round with a cord; I wonder if I can use the cord here." The only cord he had was attached to his bow. He was going to take it off when a thought struck him. He loosened the string a bit and twisted it once about his spindle. Then he drew the bow back and forth. The spindle was turned at a great rate. He saw he must hold one end with his left hand while the other rested in the hollow in the block. With his right, he drew the bow back and forth. How eagerly he worked! He had twirled but a few minutes when the dust in the hollow burst into fire from the heat produced by the rapidly twirling spindle.

Robinson was too overjoyed to make any use of it. He danced and capered about like one gone mad until the fire had gone out. But that was of no matter now, since he could get fire when he wanted it.

He hastened to make him a rude fireplace and oven of stones. He hollowed out a place in the ground and lined and covered it with large flat stones. On one side he built up a chimney to draw up the smoke and make the fire burn brightly. He brought wood and some dry fungus or mushroom. This he powdered and soon had fire caught in it. He kindled in this way the wood in his stove and soon had a hot fire.

The first thing he did in the way of cooking was to roast some rabbit meat on a spit or forked stick held in his hand over the fire. Nothing Robinson had ever eaten was to be compared to this.

"I can do many things now," thought Robinson. "My work will not be nearly so hard. My fire will be my servant and help me make my tools as well as cook my food. I can now cook my corn and rice."

XXVIII

ROBINSON MAKES BASKETS

Robinson still continued anxious about his food supply when he could no longer gather it fresh from the fields and forest. Corn had again become ripe. He had found in a wet, marshy place some wild rice-plants loaded with ripened grain. As he now had fire he only had to have some way of storing up grains and he would not lack for food. He knew that grain stored away must be kept dry and that he must especially provide against dampness in his cave or in his bower.

If he only had some baskets. These would be just the thing. But how was he to get them? Robinson had never given a thought to either material or the method of making them. He, however, was gradually acquiring skill and confidence in himself. So far he had managed to meet all his wants. He had invented tools and made his own clothes and shelter, and, "Now," said he to himself, "I will solve the new problem. I must first study the materials that I have at hand." He remembered the splint market baskets in which his father took vegetables home from the store. He recalled how the thin splints were woven.

"They went over and under," he said. "That is simple enough if I had the splints." He set himself diligently to work to find a plant whose bark or split branches could be used for splints. He tried to peel off the rough outer bark of several trees in order to examine the inner layers of soft fibrous material. He found several trees that gave promise of furnishing abundance of long, thin strips, but the labor of removing the bark with his rude imperfect tools was so great that he resolved that he would have to find some other kind of material.

"Why need the strips be flat?" he thought. "I believe I could weave them in the same way if I used the long, thin, tough willow rods I saw growing by the brookside, when I was returning from my journey."

He found on trial that the weaving went very well, but that he must have strong, thick rods or ribs running up and down to give strength and form to his basket. He worked hard, but it was slow work. It was three days before his first basket was done. He made many mistakes and was obliged many times to undo what he had accomplished in order to correct some error. And at last when he had woven the basket as large as he thought was suitable for his purpose, he did not know how to stop or finish the top so as to keep the basket from unraveling. At last he hit upon the plan of fastening two stout rods, one outside, the other inside, the basket. These he sewed firmly, over and over, to the basket with a kind of fibre from a plant he had discovered that looked almost to be what he had heard called the century plant in the parks at home.

On attempting his next basket, he thought long how he might improve and save time. He must hasten, or the now almost daily rains would destroy his ripened wild corn and rice.

"If I could use coils of that long grass I saw growing in the marsh beside the rice," he thought, "I could make twice the progress." He gathered an armful, twisted it into cables about an inch thick and wove it into his frame of upright rods instead of the horizontal layer of willow canes. This answered his purpose just as well and rendered the making of large baskets the work of a few hours. He found, however, that the willow rods or osiers were not pliant enough to work well in fastening his coils of grass cables together. He tried several things and at last succeeded best when he used the long thread-like fibre of the century-like plant. He had, however, to make a stout framework of rods. He would first coil his grass rope into this frame and then sew it together with twine or thread made from this fibre.

He afterwards tried making smaller and finer baskets out of the fibre that he had discovered, which could be easily had from the thick-leaved plant he thought he had seen at home. He first used long, tough, fine roots he had seen when digging up the tree at the mouth of his cave. Afterwards he discovered some tall, tough reeds growing near by. He laid in a supply of these. He found that when he wanted to use them, a good soaking in water made them as pliable and tough as when first cut.

The making of the baskets and storing up grains made it possible for Robinson to become a farmer and thus make himself independent. This thought was a great relief to him.

XXIX

ROBINSON BECOMES A FARMER

Robinson had now been on the island long enough to know how the seasons changed. He found that there were two kinds of weather there, wet weather and dry weather. There were two wet seasons in each year and two dry ones. During the wet seasons, which lasted nearly three months, Robinson had to remain pretty closely at home, and could not gather grain, for the plants were then starting from the seeds. It ripened in the dry seasons. Robinson soon found that he must have a store of corn and wild rice for food during the rainy seasons. He, however, knew nothing about planting and harvesting, nor preparing the ground for seed.

He had it all to learn with no teacher or books to instruct him. He found a little space near his dwelling free from trees and thought he would plant some corn seed here. He did not know the proper time for planting. He thought because it was warm, seed would grow at any time. It happened his first seed was put in at the beginning of the dry season. He watched and waited to rejoice his eyes with the bright green of sprouting corn, but the seed did not grow. There was no rain and the sun's heat parched the land till it was dry and hard on the upland where his corn was planted.

"Very well," thought Robinson, "I will plant it at the beginning of the wet season, either in March or September." He did so; the seed quickly sprouted up. But the weeds, shrubs, and vines sprouted as quickly, and before Robinson was aware, his corn was overgrown and choked out by a rank growth of weeds and vines.

"I see," said Robinson, "that I must thoroughly prepare the soil before planting my seed." But he had no spade and no other tool that would stand the strain of digging among tough matted roots. But he must succeed. He put a new handle in the stone hoe or pick he had already made. His mussel shell spade was worn out. He must set himself to fashion out another. He decided to make one from the tough heavy wood of a tree that grew plentifully in the forest.

55

He was lucky enough to find a tree of this kind whose bole had been split lengthwise by the falling of an old rotten tree near it. With his stone tools and the help of fire he managed after several days' work to make a wide sharpened tool out of one of the large pieces split off. It was a little over three feet long. He had trimmed one end small and cut notches in the sides about one foot from the flat end. He could place his foot in the notch and thrust his wooden spade into the earth. With his rude tool he dug up and turned the soil of a small space of ground several times to kill the vines and weeds. His corn quickly sprouted after this attempt and outstripped the weeds and vines which Robinson constantly had to hold in check by pulling and hoeing. He was rejoiced at his growing crop and went each morning to feast his eyes on the rapidly expanding leaves and ears.

One morning as he came in sight of the little clearing he thought he saw something disappearing in the low brush on the other side as he approached. Alas, his labor had been in vain! A herd of wild goats had found out the place and had utterly destroyed his crop. Robinson sat down nearby and surveyed the ruin of his little field. "It is plain," thought he, "I will have to fence in the field or I will never be able to harvest my crop. I cannot watch it all the time."

He had already learned from his experience in making the fence around the goat pasture that the branches of many kinds of shrubs and trees, when broken off and thrust into the ground, will send out roots and leaves and at length if planted close together in a line, will form a thick hedge which no kind of beast can get through or over. He found out some willow trees whose branches broke easily, and soon had enough to thrust into the ground about six inches apart around the entire edge of his little field, which contained about one eighth of an acre.

After this hedge had grown so as to be a fair protection to his crop he tried planting again at the proper season. He spaded up the ground and pulled out the matted roots as best he could and with great pains and care planted his corn in straight even rows. To make them straight and each hill of corn the same distance from its neighbors, he first marked off the ground in squares whose sides were about three and one half feet long.

"Now," thought he, "I will reap the reward of my labor." The corn grew rapidly, and toward the end of the first dry season was filling out and ripening its ears. But to Robinson's dismay a new danger threatened his crop against which he could not fence. He was in despair. The birds were fast eating and destroying his partially ripened corn. He could not husk it yet. It was not ripe enough. He thought how easy it would be to protect his field if he had a gun. But he had learned that it is useless to give time to idle dreaming. He must do something and that quick.

"If I could catch some of these rascals," he thought, "I would hang them up on poles, dead, as a warning to the rest." It seemed almost a hopeless task, but he went about it. It was in vain he tried to kill some of them by throwing rocks and sticks. He could not get near enough to them. At length he laid snares and succeeded in snaring three birds. He had learned to weave a pliable, strong thong out of cocoa and other fibre that he was now acquainted with. The birds thus caught he fastened on broken branches of trees which he stuck into the earth in different parts of his field. The birds heeded the warning and visited his corn field no more that season.

At the end of the season he gathered or husked his corn and after it was thoroughly dry he shelled it from the cob with his hands. He used his baskets in which to carry his husked ears from the field to his cave and in which to store it when shelled. He found that the ears were larger and better filled and plumper than when the plants grew wild. He selected the largest and best filled ears for his seed the next time. In this way his new crop of corn was always better in kind and yielded more than the old one.

At first he grew two crops a year, but by experimenting he found out about how much he needed for his own use and planted once a year enough to give him a liberal supply.

He observed that the wild rice grew in swampy lands, so that he did not make the mistake of trying to raise it upon the upland where the corn grew best. He saw at once that the planting of rice on low, marshy or wet land was beyond his present strength and tools. "Some time in the future," he thought, "I may try it."

Robinson also found wild grapes in abundance. These he dried by hanging them on the branches of trees. He thus had a store of raisins for each rainy season.

XXX

ROBINSON AS POTTER

Robinson was now anxious to cook his food, to boil his rice and vegetables and bake bread, but he could do nothing without cooking vessels. He had tried to use cocoanut shells, but these were too small and there was no way to keep them from falling over and spilling the contents. He determined to try to make some clay vessels. He knew where he could get a kind of clay that had the appearance of making good ware. It was fine grained and without lumps or pebbles. He was much perplexed to mould the clay into right shapes. He tried taking a lump and shaping it into a vessel with his hands. He tried many times, but each time the clay broke and he was forced to try some other way. He recalled how he had made his basket out of strands of twisted grass and wondered whether he could not make his pots in the same way.

He spun the clay out into a long rope and began to coil it around a small basket forming the layers together with his hands. This was easy, but he did not see clearly how he was going to get the basket out from the inside of the pot. He found he could copy in this way any form he wished, but he finally hit upon the plan of making a form of wicker work and coiling the clay rope inside it, for he saw that whether he succeeded or not in getting the clay free from the basket he could use the pot, and besides if the pot would stand the fire the basket would burn off. To dry the pots Robinson stood them in the sun a few days. When they were dry he tried to cook some soup in one of them. He filled it with water and put it on his stove or oven, but how sadly had he deceived himself. In a short time the water soaked into the clay and soon the pot had fallen to pieces.

"How foolish I am!" said Robinson to himself; "the pots have to be fired before they can be used." He set about this at once. He found two stones of equal size, placed them near each other and laid a third across these. He then placed three large pots upon them and made a hot fire under them. No sooner had the flame shot up than one of the pots cracked in two. "I probably made the fire too hot at first," thought Robinson.

He drew out some of the coals and wood, but afterwards gradually increased the fire again. He could not, however, get the pots hot enough to turn red He brought the dryest and hardest wood, but could not succeed in getting them hot enough to turn red. At length he was tired out and was compelled to give it up. When the pots were cool he tried to boil water in one. It was no better than the sun dried one. He saw that he must provide some way to get the pots much hotter than he could in the open air He resolved to make an oven of stones large enough to take in the wood as well as the pots. It must be above ground so that there might be plenty of draught for the fire. With great labor, he pried up and carried together flat stones enough to make an oven about four feet high with a chimney at one side. He had put in the center a stone table on which he could place three quite large pots. He left an opening in one side that could be partially closed by a large, flat stone.

He worked eagerly and at the end of the second day he was ready to fire his oven. He first carried together a good quantity of dry wood, then he put in his pots and laid the wood around them. In a short time he had a very hot fire. He kept this up all day and until late at night.

The next morning he went to his oven and found his pots were a beautiful red. He drew out the fire and allowed them to cool slowly. Then he filled one with water and set it over the fire to heat it. Before many minutes the water was boiling and Robinson had another reason to be thankful. He wept for joy. His patient labors had brought their rewards. No prince could feel as happy as Robinson now. He had overcome all difficulties. Starting with nothing but his hands, he was now able to supply all his wants. "If I only had a companion now," he thought, "I would have nothing further to wish as long as I stay on the island."

XXXI

ROBINSON AS BAKER

Now that Robinson had fire, he determined to try to make bread. He had seen the servants at home make bread many times, but he had not observed closely and knew next to nothing about the way bread is made. He knew he must in some way grind the corn into flour, but how could he do this? He had no mill nor any tools with which to crush the corn.

He first tried to find a stone large and hard enough out of which he might hollow a vessel or kind of mortar. He thought he could put the corn into this mortar and grind it by means of another stone or pestle. It was with great difficulty that he could get a stone of suitable size and form. After several days' trial he at last got one cut out from some layers of rock near the shore. He made a hollow place in it. Then he took a smaller oblong shaped rock for his pestle.

He took great pride in these new tools. "I shall soon be a stone-cutter," he said to himself, "as well as a farmer and potter." But his stone mortar was a failure. The rock was too soft. Every time he thrust the pestle down, it loosened small pieces of the stone vessel. These mixed with the ground corn or flour and made it unfit to eat. There was no way to separate the sand from the crushed grain.

He resolved then to try to make a mortar and pestle of hard wood. Now that he had fire, he could do this, though it cost him many a hard day's work. He found not far away a log of very hard wood. By building a fire at the right distance from one end he was able to separate a piece of the log. He rolled this to his cave and made a good-sized hollow in it by burning. This pestle was not so difficult to make. He took a limb or branch of an ironwood tree, burned it in two at the place to make it the right length. By burning also he rounded one end and then he was ready for the grinding. After cleaning his mortar and pestle carefully he placed some corn in the hollow and soon had some fine yellow meal or flour without any grit or sand in it.

His next care was to separate the coarse outer husk or covering of the kernel from the finer parts that make the meal. He had no sieve.

His net was too coarse. It let both bran and meal go through. "I must make a net or cloth fine enough to sift or bolt my flour," said he. Such was now his skill in spinning and weaving that this was not hard to do. He had soon woven in his loom a piece of fine netting which allowed the meal to shake through, but held back the coarse bran or outer husk of the kernel. Out of the dry corn that he had stored up he now made quite a quantity of flour. This he kept tightly covered in a large earthen pot or jar that he had made for this purpose. "I must keep all my food clean and protect it from the ants and other insects as well as dust and damp," he thought.

His preparations were now nearly made. He had already his stove of flat stones. On this he could set his pots to boil water, cook rice, and meat, but it would not do for baking a loaf of bread of any thickness. He must have an oven or enclosed place into which he could put the loaf to bake it. By the use of flat stones he soon rebuilt his stove so as to have an oven that did fine service. Now it was mixing the dough that claimed his attention. He had of course no yeast to make raised or light bread. He poured goats' milk on the flour and kneaded it into a thick dough. He did not forget to add salt. He placed his loaf in a shallow earthen pan he had made for this purpose. After the fire had heated the stones of his oven through, he put in his loaf and soon was enjoying a meal of corn bread and meat stew.

Robinson soon tried to make cocoa from the beans of the cocoa palm that grew in the island. This with good rich goats' milk in it he thought the best drink in the world. He often thought of making sugar from the sugar cane plant he had discovered in the island. But the labor of squeezing out the juice was too great. He could think of no way to do this without the help of horses or oxen.

XXXII

ROBINSON AS FISHERMAN

Robinson was now eager to use his fire and cooking vessels. He had noticed with hungry eyes fine large fish in the creek near his cave. But he had never taken the trouble to catch any. "What is the use?" he thought. "I cannot eat them raw." It was different now and he began to devise ways of making a catch. How he longed for a fish-hook, such as he had so often used when loitering along the Hudson River! "But a fish-hook is not to be thought of," he said to himself, "unless I can make one of bone." He went down to the brook and searched long for a fish-bone that he might make use of for this purpose. He found nothing.

"I must try something else," he thought. He remembered the nets he used to see along the Hudson and wondered if he could not make a small one to pull through the water and thus catch the fish.

He had now a better source of fibre for weaving and for spinning into lines and ropes. He had discovered this when he was trying to find a good strong thread or yarn with which to bind the coils of his grass-made baskets together. He obtained fibre in great abundance from the century-like plant. He found if he broke off the long leaves of this plant and allowed them to decay there remained a long, tough fibrous substance out of which strong cords could be twisted or yarn made for weaving a coarse cloth or netting.

Out of this he spun yarn thread to make a net about three or four feet by two feet. He fastened cords to four corners of this, tied them to a long pole, and was now prepared to test his plan for catching fish.

The brook he found was too shallow for him to catch fish in this way. At the sight of him and his net, they scurried away to deep water. Neither could he succeed in the shallow water along the shore. "I must wade out as far as I can," he said to himself, "and draw the net through the water."

As he did this he was surprised at the many forms of sea life, new to him, that he saw. He, however, was careful and watchful. He

63

walked along near the shore to a point where some, rocks showed above the surface. As he looked ahead he saw the single eye of a giant cuttle-fish glaring at him from among the rocks. It was thrusting out its long arms towards him. He drew back quickly, but as he did so he was terrified to hear the snap of some huge creature's jaws near him. A great shark had seen him and had thrown himself on his back to seize him in his rows of sharp teeth, but was prevented reaching him by the shallowness of the water.

Robinson was too much terrified to continue longer his attempt at fishing. He went back to his cave with only a few small ones, not worth the trouble of dressing for his dinner.

The next day undismayed he tried again. He succeeded in drawing in some very beautiful large fish. Their sides shone as burnished gold and silver. "Now," he thought, "I will have a feast." He carried them home, carefully cleaned and dressed them, seasoned them with his salt, and broiled them over his fire. Imagine his disappointment when they proved unfit to eat. Their flesh was coarse and tough and ill-tasting. He saw that the catching of fish for his table was a more difficult thing than he thought it. He must not only catch fish, but catch ones that could be eaten. He could only tell the good from the bad by trying them.

He was more fortunate in his next venture. He was going along the shore at the mouth of the creek which ran near his cave when he noticed a group of fishes, dark bluish above with silvery sides. The largest of them were about two feet long. They were feeding on the bottom in the brackish water at the mouth of the creek, which at its mouth opened out into quite a little bay or inlet. They would take up a mouthful of earth from the bottom and let it wash through their mouths, keeping all the bits of food that happened to be in it. When one fish got a good place to feed the others swam around it and tried to get some of the food.

Robinson watched his chance and slipped his net under a group, while each one was busy trying to get the best mouthful of mud. He drew up three quite large fish, but just as he was about to lift them from the water, one of the cords which bound the net to the poles broke and he saw his catch fall back into the creek and dart away in the deepest water. But Robinson was not to be discouraged. He soon mended his net and at last was successful. In a short time he drew out another catch of two fish.

These proved excellent food and were so abundant as to furnish Robinson with all the fish he wanted as long as he stayed on the island.

XXXIII

ROBINSON BUILDS A BOATt

Robinson had wished for a boat many times. He wished to explore the shore of his island. He wanted to go clear around it so that he might see it on every side. But he knew the work of making a boat would be great, if not wholly impossible.

The shaping of boards to build a boat with his rude tools was not to be thought of. He knew how the Indians made boats out of bark of trees. But he saw that for his purpose so light a boat would not do. He finally remembered a second Indian way of making a boat by hollowing out a large log. The forest was full of the boles of trees that had been blown down. But they were far away from the shore. At first he did not think of this very much. He had overcome so many difficulties that he thought, "Never mind, I will get my boat to water, no matter where I make it, in some way." So he selected a tree trunk some distance from the bank of the little creek near his cave and began work.

He had first to burn out his log the proper length and hack it into boat shape with his stone tools. This was very slow and tedious work. He had to handle the fire with great care for there was always the danger of spoiling the shape of the slowly forming boat. Both ends must be sharpened, but one more than the other to form the prow or forward going end. After he had shaped his boat, he began hollowing it out. This he did also by burning for the most part. He used the branches of pitch bearing trees for this purpose. But it was so slow. He worked at his boat all the time he could spare from his regular duties in attending to his goats, his garden and his cave. He was always making his cave larger. Every time he made a piece of furniture or stored away grain he must make more room in his cave by digging away the earth and carrying it out. He had made a large strong wicker basket for this purpose.

He had had a vague idea that when he got his boat done he would dig a trench back from the bank of the creek and thus float his boat. But he had not thought it out clearly. "Or anyway," he thought, "I can in some way manage to roll it to the water." He must now actually plan to put some of these ideas into effect. He first went over the ground and found that to dig a trench from the water to the boat, so that the water would come to the boat, he would have to dig it twenty feet deep. "I can never do this," he said, "with my poor tools."

He next tried his rolling plan. But he had been so anxious to have a large boat that he had overlooked everything else. Try as hard as he might he could not stir his boat from the spot. After many trials with the longest levers he could handle, the boat still stuck fast. It would not budge an inch. He at last gave it up. "It will lie here," he thought, "to remind me how foolish it is to attempt to do anything without first having thought it out carefully."

There was nothing to do but to choose another tree trunk. This time he selected a much smaller one, and one that lay at the top of the little slope or incline from the bank of the creek. After another weary six months of work he had his second boat ready for launching. With a good stout lever he gave it a start, when it rolled quickly down into the water. Robinson again wept for joy. Of all his projects this had cost him the most work and pains and at last to see his plans successful filled him with delight.

The next problem was how to make it go. He had no certain knowledge how far it was around the island, but he knew it was farther than he wanted to row or paddle his boat. Yet he knew from the way the wind blew that he could not always depend upon a sail to help him. He must become skillful in paddling his boat. A sail too would be very helpful at times. He imagined how pleasant it would be sitting in the boat sailing along with a gentle wind. "When the wind is favorable," he thought, "I will only have to steer with my paddle."

So he set about weaving a sail of his sisal fibre. To do this he had to make a much larger loom than he had yet used. His sail must be at least four feet square. He was now so skilled in weaving that this was soon finished. He then made plenty of string, cord, and rope, put in a mast and was ready to sail. But he did not venture far away until he had spent weeks and weeks in learning to steer, sail, and paddle his boat.

XXXIV

ROBINSON AS A SAILOR

Ever since Robinson had finished his boat he had been eager to make a tour of his island. He had indeed made a journey by land. But the deep forests and tangled vines made it very difficult to travel. His journeys had shown him but a small part of the land. He wished to know all about the land of which he, so far as he knew, was the sole master.

His first care was to fit up his boat with provisions. He made some large baskets in which to carry food and a large covered jar for water. These he stored in the bow and the stern of his boat. He fastened his parasol on the stern for a shelter from the sun. He baked up a quantity of cakes or loaves of bread and packed them in his baskets. He had woven these so carefully that they would almost hold water.

At last all was ready. It was on the sixth day of November in the sixth year of his life on the island that Robinson hoisted his sail and set out upon this voyage of discovery. He had waited until the wind was gentle and blowing as far easterly as it does at that place. He scudded along bravely, running with the land toward the East and North. All went well until he came to a low reef or ledge of rocks running far out to sea in a north-easterly direction.

When Robinson observed this he went on shore and climbed to a high point to see if it was safe to venture. He was afraid of hidden currents, or streams of water. These might carry him away from the shore and prevent him from getting around the point.

He did indeed observe that there was a current running out to sea past the ledge, but he thought he could by careful paddling keep his boat from striking the rock. If he could once get beyond the ledge, the wind would help him double or get around the point. Indeed the danger was that the wind would blow him on to the rocks.

He waited for two days for a gentle wind. At last without sail he pushed his boat into the current and was born swiftly seaward. He found the current much stronger than he thought it would be. It rushed his frail boat on past the point of the rocks and out into the sea. Try as best he might he could not change its course. He was steadily going out to sea. He gave himself up for lost. He reproached himself for being so rash and foolhardy as to trust his fortunes in so frail a craft. How dear at this time seemed the island to him! The wind which he had depended on to help him at this point had died down so that it was at the mercy of the current. He kept urging his boat to the westward as much as possible, with all his strength, hoping that a breeze would finally spring up.

He struggled on bravely until about noon. He had been carried out a great distance into the sea, but not so far as to lose sight of the land. All at once he felt the breeze freshening up. It caught his sail and soon his boat was cutting across the current. He did not have to go far before he was free from it and making headway for the island, which he reached about four o'clock in the afternoon.

He found himself on the northern shore of the island, but before long the shore ran away to the southward again. He ran briskly along the west side until he found a little bay or cove. He determined to enter this, draw up his boat on shore and make his way back home across the island on foot. He was almost exhausted with his great labor and was worn out with anxiety.

In the centre of the arms of the cove he found a little creek entering the sea. He paddled into this and found a good place to hide his boat.

As soon as Robinson was again on land he fell on his knees and with tears in his eyes thanked God for his deliverance. The island which had seemed to him a prison now seemed the fairest and dearest place in the world.

Having made his boat safe he started back toward his shelter. But he was too tired to go far. He soon came to a little grove of trees beneath which he laid himself down and soon was fast asleep.

You can imagine with what surprise Robinson was awakened out of his sleep by a voice calling his name. "Robinson, Robinson Crusoe," it said, "poor Robinson Crusoe! Where are you Robinson, where have you been?"

He was so fast asleep that he did not at first rouse up entirely and thought he was dreaming. But the voice kept calling, "Robinson, Robinson, poor Robinson Crusoe!" He was greatly frightened and started up. But no sooner were his eyes opened than he saw his parrot sitting on a branch of a tree. He knew at once the source of the voice.

Polly had missed her master and was also exploring the island. It was a pleasant surprise. She immediately flew to him and lit on his shoulder. She showed in many ways how glad she was to see him and kept saying, "Poor Robinson, poor Robinson Crusoe!"

Robinson remained here over night and the next morning made his way back to the shelter. Up to this time Robinson had never seen any dangerous animals on the island. He had grown used to life there and went about without fear of animals. But as he was returning across a little opening, he saw a clump of palms in the centre of the opening, swaying about. He did not at first see what caused this, but soon there was thrust out the head of a great serpent. Its jaws were open and its eyes were fixed on a poor terrified little rabbit. The rabbit seemed rooted to the spot. It could not stir a muscle and was soon caught in the folds of the great snake.

This sight made Robinson greatly afraid. He wanted to rush to the rescue of the rabbit, but what could he do against such a foe? He resolved in the future to keep a more careful watch and always to sleep in his bower.

Robinson had enough of exploring for some time. He was contented to remain at home. He made many things he needed. He had saved all the skins of the goats he had killed for meat and all that had died from any cause. These he made into rugs for his bed. He kept at his loom too, for he was anxious to weave enough of his coarse cloth to make him a suit of clothes. He learned how to braid mats and rugs out of his fibre, and finally replaced his awkward hat and parasol with others braided very skillfully from the long grasses that grew so abundantly in the marshy places.

Another thing that Robinson was now able to make or weave out of his fibre was a hammock. He had slept all this time on a bed made of poles laid lengthwise and thickly covered with the skins of goats and rabbits.

Now he could have a comfortable place to sleep. He did not stop until he had made two. One was for the bower and the other was for use out-of-doors. When his work was done in the evening or in the heat of the midday he would lie in it at full length under the shade of the trees.

XXXV

A DISCOVERY

Robinson could not forget his boat. It seemed a companion. "It may be the means of my escape from this place," he thought. He took frequent journeys across the island to where his little boat lay in the cove. He would start out in the morning and walk over to the west side of the island, take his boat and have a pleasant little sail. He always returned home before dark, for to tell the truth, Robinson was a coward. He was as timid as a hare. He was afraid of everything and spent many nights without sleep because of fear.

It was while on one of his visits to his boat that Robinson made a discovery that changed his whole life. It happened one day, about noon, when he was going toward his boat that he, with great surprise, saw the print of a man's naked foot on the shore in the sand. He stood like one rooted to the ground. He could not move, so great was his surprise and fear. He listened, looked around, but could hear and see nothing. He went up to a little hill to look further, but nothing was in sight. There was but the one footprint. There was no doubt about it, there it was, foot, toes, heel and every part of a foot. Robinson tried to think how it might have gotten there, but he could not. It was a mystery. He was greatly afraid and started at once for his shelter. He ran like one pursued. At every little way he would look behind to see if anyone was following him.

Never a frightened rabbit ran to his hiding place with more terror than Robinson ran to his cave. He did not sleep that night for fear and remained in his shelter for three days, never venturing out. But his food was growing short and his goats needed to be milked. He finally with a thousand wild fancies forced himself to go about his duties.

But he could not get the footprint out of his mind. He spent many sad and fearful days thinking about it. "How could it have gotten there? Whose was it? Was the owner savage or not? What did he want on the island?" were some of the questions that haunted him.

"Perhaps," he thought one day, "I just imagined I saw a footprint, or perhaps it was one of my own that I have made when going to sail my boat." He took courage at this and began to go about the island again. But he went in great fear, always looking behind him. He was always ready to run at the first sign of danger. He had made himself a large, strong, new bow and plenty of arrows. He carried these in a quiver he had made from his cloth. He fashioned too a sharp-pointed, lance-like weapon which he hurled with a kind of sling. In his belt he carried some new sharpened stone knives. He had found a better kind of rock out of which to make his knives. It resembled glass and could be brought to a fine, keen edge.

Armed thus, he began to have more confidence. He had a strong desire to see the footprint again and make up his mind about it. He wished to measure it. In this way he could tell certainly whether it was a chance print of his own foot or not. So, after a few days, he again ventured across the island. Alas, on measuring the print it was much larger than his own! There could no longer be any doubt that it belonged to someone else.

Again great fear fell on poor Robinson. He shook with cold and fright.
He resolved to make himself more secure against attack.

He cut and carried willow stakes and set them in a thick hedge around in front of his shelter. This was outside the first and enclosed it. In a season or two these had grown to such a height as to shut out all view of his home from sight to one coming to it from the front.

His flock of goats gave him many troubled thoughts. His goats were his greatest treasure. From them he obtained without trouble his meat, his milk and butter.

"What if they were discovered and killed or carried away?" He resolved to divide his herd into three parts and secrete these in separate fenced pastures in different parts of the island. His herd of goats now numbered twenty-five. He made thorough search about the island for the most secluded and best hidden spots where he could fence in a pasture.

One day as he was exploring on the west side of the island to find another open space for a goat field, he thought he spied away out to sea a boat. He looked long and anxiously and yet he was not sure that it was a boat he saw. But how easy, thought Robinson, for the people of the mainland, which must be at no great distance to the westward, to come across to this side of the island in fair weather. He thought too, how fortunate he was to have been cast on the east side of the island. For there he had his shelter in the very safest part.

As he was coming down from a hill where he had gone to get a better view of the sea he made another discovery. About him everywhere at the foot of the hill were bones of all kinds. Near by too, were charcoal and ashes. There could be no mistake, the place was visited by human beings. These were very likely savages. Everything showed that they came for the purpose of feasting and not for plundering. It was very likely that they neither sought anything on the island nor expected it.

This thought greatly relieved Robinson. He returned home in a very thankful and composed state of mind. He had now been on the island almost eighteen years and had not been discovered. Yet, no doubt, the island had been visited many times by the savages since he had been there.

In a short time his fear of discovery wore off and he began to live just as he did before his discovery.

He took, however, greater precaution against surprise. He always carried his bow and arrows, his lance and knives. He was also very careful about making a great smoke from his fire. He burned a great quantity of wood in a pit and made charcoal. With this material he had a fine fire with a very little smoke. Every day also he went to the top of the hill back of his shelter in order to discover if possible the approach of savages.

XXXVI

THE LANDING OF THE SAVAGES

Another year passed by, Robinson longed more and more to get away from the island. Year after year he had hoped and watched in vain for a passing ship. Every day he would scan the waters that held him prisoner for the welcome sight of a sail. He had been disappointed. Now his only hope was to escape to the mainland in some way. He feared the savages. He had heard stories of their being cannibals. But if they could come to his island in their canoes against the prevailing wind, why could he not get to the mainland with it in his favor?

Strange as it may be, Robinson began to wish for the return of the savages. He hoped to watch them at a distance and find out something about their customs. More especially he wished that he might capture one of them. He had two reasons for this. In the first place he would have a companion. He pictured fondly how he would teach him gentle manners and the English speech. And, too, the companion would be able to help him. Besides this he longed above all to know more of the mainland and whether it would be safe to go there. He wanted to find out in what kind of boat they made the voyage. He thought that if he had such a person he would have someone to show him the way to reach the land.

The more he thought, the more anxious he became to see the savages on the island. He thought so much about it by day that he dreamed about it at night. One night he dreamed that the savages came, drew their boats upon the shore and began to prepare their feast. As he watched them one of their number broke away from his fellows and came straight toward his hiding-place. Robinson thought he rushed out, drove away those that followed the fleeing man and rescued him. This dream made a deep impression upon him and made him await the coming of the savages with great hopes and eagerness.

It was more than eighteen months after he had formed this plan of capturing one of the savages before the savages made their appearance. Robinson was surprised one morning to see no less than five canoes drawn up on the shore at a point on his side of the island about two miles below his shelter, to the south. The people that had come in them were on shore and out of sight. Robinson went back to his shelter to make his plans. He made up his mind that he would be foolish to attack them. There must be twenty-five or thirty of them. He finally went to a point where he could see farther inland and soon caught sight of a crowd of about thirty savages. They were naked and dancing around and around in a circle. All the while they were singing and making hideous noises. There was a fire in the center of the ring of savages. "They are cooking their feast," thought Robinson. "Maybe I can surprise them while they eat and rush in and seize one." But this seemed too great a risk to run. He had no weapons but his bow and arrows, his lance and knife. What could he do against so great a number?

But fortune favored his plans. As he gazed at them from his safe distance he saw one of their number break away from the rest and run with utmost speed directly toward his hiding-place. At once two other savages pursued him. They had no weapons but clubs. They ran with great swiftness, but the man in front was steadily gaining ground.

Robinson now to tell the truth was dreadfully frightened to see the savage run directly toward him and his shelter. He kept his place, however, and watched the race. The man running away ran along the shore and would soon come to the little creek that emptied into the sea below his home. Robinson saw that the savage would have to swim this to escape. He ran down thither and concealed himself behind a tree and waited for the fugitive to come up. As he did so, the fleeing savage plunged in and swam across with a few strong strokes. When he was well on the bank, Robinson presented himself and made signs to him to come to him and he would help him. The savage was at first almost overcome with astonishment and fright, for Robinson presented a very unusual sight. The savage at once ran to him and fell down at his feet. Indeed so great was his fright and distress that he placed one of Robinson's feet upon his neck in sign that he yielded up his life into his hands. Robinson raised him up and motioned for him to take the lance and help in defence against the men, now coming up. They hid behind trees and waited for them to swim across the stream. But this they did not do. When they reached the creek, they could see nothing of their runaway. They very slowly turned and went back to their companions.

Robinson was well content not to let them know that there was any one on the island. He feared they might return and destroy his shelter and fields.

Robinson took the savage to his shelter and gave him bread and raisins to eat, and a cup of water to drink. He was very hungry and ate greedily. After he had eaten, Robinson made signs for him to lie down and sleep, for the Indian was nearly tired out with his long and swift run.

He was a handsome fellow of his race. His limbs were large, straight and strong. He had a good face. His hair was long and black, his forehead high, and his eyes bright. His skin was not black, but of an olive color. His teeth were fine set and as white as ivory.

He slept about an hour; when he awoke he came running to Robinson and again made signs to him that he was his slave. "You saved my life," he seemed to say, "and now I will serve you." Robinson named him Friday at once, for that was the day on which the great event of his escape had taken place.

Robinson's next care was to fit him out with some clothing. He had by this time several suits made of his coarse cloth. He soon had Friday dressed in one of the old ones, with a straw or braided hat on his head. He did not think it safe to allow Friday to sleep with him in the bower. He made a little tent for him inside the enclosure. This was covered with goatskins and made a very good protection from both heat and rain.

Robinson took care to keep all his knives and weapons near him in the bower. But his fears that Friday might harm him were unfounded. Friday from the first was faithful to his master. He was sweet and obedient in all things. He seemed to look upon Robinson with the love of a child for its father and never tired of serving him.

XXXVII

ROBINSON AS A TEACHER

(From Robinson's Diary)

"I began to consider that having now two mouths to feed instead of one, I must provide more ground for my harvest and plant a larger quantity of corn than I used to plant. So I marked out a larger piece of land and began to fence it in. Friday worked not only very willingly but very hard. I told him that it was for corn to make more bread because he was now with me. He let me know that he was grateful for my kindness and would work much harder if I would tell him what to do.

"This was the pleasantest year of all the life I led in this place. Friday began to talk pretty well and understood the names of almost all the things that I called for and of all the places which I wished to send him. I was careful to teach him all the things I knew. I showed him how to plant and harvest corn, how to gather fibre, spin yarn and to weave it into cloth. He learned these things quickly and became very skillful in making pots. He knew something about this because at home he had seen the women make them. He ornamented them with figures of birds and flowers. I taught him about the true God. But as for writing he could never do much with this. I had no books and could not make him understand the importance of writing. He began to talk a great deal to me. This delighted me very much. I began to love him exceedingly. He was so very honest and faithful.

"After I had taught him English I tried one day to find out whether he had any wish to return to his own country and as I talked to him about it I saw his face light up with joy and his eye sparkle. From this I had no doubt but that Friday would like to be in his own country again. This for a time made me sad, to think how eagerly he would leave me to be among his savage friends. 'Do you not wish you were back in your own country, Friday?' I said to him one day. 'Yes,' he said, 'I be much O glad to be back in my country.' 'What would you do there,' said I? 'Would you turn wild again and do as the savages do?' He shook his head and said very gravely, 'No, no, Friday tell them to live good. He tell them to plant corn and live like white mans.'

"One day when we were on the top of a hill on the west side of the island, Friday suddenly began to jump and dance about in great glee. I asked him what the matter was. 'O, joy, O glad,' he said; 'there my country!' The air was so clear that from this place, as I had before discovered, land could be distinctly seen looking westward.

"I asked him how far it was from our island to his country and whether their canoes were ever lost in coming and going. He said that there was no danger. No canoes were ever wrecked and that it was easy to get back and forth. I asked him many things about his people and country. He told me that away to the west of his country there lived 'white mans like you.' I thought these must be the people of Central America, and asked him how I might come from this island and get among these white men. He made me understand that I must have a large boat as big as two canoes.

"I resolved at once to begin to make a boat large enough for us to pass over to the land we could see lying to the west and if possible to go on to the white man's country Friday told me about. It took us nearly two months to make our boat and rig her out with sails, masts, rudder, and anchor. We had to weave our sails and twist our rope. We burned out the canoe from a large fallen log. We used a great stone tied securely to the end of a strong rope for an anchor.

"When we had the boat in the water, Friday showed great skill in rowing or paddling it.

"He had managed boats ever since he was old enough, but he did not know how to handle a sail or rudder. He learned very quickly, however, to sail and steer the boat and soon was perfectly at home in it.

"We made our boat safe by keeping it in the little cove at the mouth of the creek. I had Friday to fetch rocks and build a dock or place for landing. But the rainy season was now coming on and we must wait for fair weather. In the meantime I planned to lay by such quantities of food as we would need to take along."

XXXVIII

ANOTHER SHIPWRECK

One evening Robinson sat in his shelter thinking of his plans to escape to Friday's country. He was sad. For, after all, this place was very dear to him. It was the only home he had. Had he not made everything with his own hands? It was doubly dear to him on this account. He thought how it would grieve him to leave his goats, his fields, and the many comforts he had here.

He had been telling Friday of his home in New York. He told him of the great city, and of its many wonderful sights. He told him of his country and people, of his flag and its history. All these things brought back memories of his boyhood and he wondered what changes had come in his long absence. Friday, with wonderful intelligence, listened to all Robinson told him. He was delighted in hearing Robinson tell of the wonders of the great world, for he had never known anything about it. As they talked Robinson noticed the approach of a storm. The sky was getting black with clouds. The winds were blowing a hurricane. The waves were coming in mountain high. It reminded him of the eventful night now twenty-five years ago when his ship was tossed up on the shore like an egg shell and broken to pieces.

Suddenly there was a sound that made Robinson start from his seat with the wildest alarm. Was it the sound of a cannon from the ocean or the terrible crash and roar of the water on the rocks of the coast? There it is again; it is a cannon! Some ship is in distress! This is its signal! Robinson ran out and down to the shore with Friday at his heels.

"O master!" said Friday, "can we not help? If they only knew the island was here and how to steer into the harbor beyond the point of land on the south."

Robinson was so excited that he scarcely knew what he was doing. He ran up and down the shore calling wildly, but the awful roar of the sea and wind drowned his cries. Suddenly his thoughts came to him. "Quick, Friday, get some fire in a pot. We will run to the point, gather grass and wood, and make a fire there. Maybe we can guide them into the harbor."

They soon had a great beacon light sending its welcome greeting far over the sea. The pilot of the ship saw it and steered his ship nearer and nearer. Robinson was ready to shout for joy as the ship seemed about to make the harbor. The ship had her sails torn in shreds and her rudder broken. It was hard to steer her in such a gale. On rounding the point, she was blown on the rocks. With a frightful crash which could be heard above the din of the storm she struck and held fast. Robinson could hear the cries of the men and the orders of the officers. They were trying to get boats ready to put off, but such was the confusion of the storm and the enormous waves breaking over the deck that it could not be done quickly. Before the men could get a boat into the sea, and get into it, the ship gave a lurch to one side as though about to sink. All the men jumped for one boat. It was overburdened. The wind tossed it about. The sea soon filled it and it went down and all were lost.

Robinson and Friday remained on the shore all night. They watched to see if they could not help some poor sailor that might cling to a plank and be blown on shore. They saw no one.

At last they lay down, but they could not sleep. Many times they sprang up and ran about for fear that some poor fellow would need their help. At last morning came. The storm ceased. Robinson and Friday searched everywhere for the bodies of the sailors, but could find none. But the wind had blown the ship in plain view, and into shallow waters. It was lying on the bottom with more than half its bulk out of the water. The masts were gone. It was a sad sight. No human being could be seen on it.

They were now rejoiced that they had their boat ready. "Let us take it," said Robinson "and go out to the ship. It may be some person is still on the unfortunate ship." They were soon by the ship's side. They rowed around it until they saw a rope hanging down from the deck. Robinson seized this and clambered up. Friday tied the boat fast, and followed. Robinson opened the door leading from the deck into the ship and went down. He searched in all the cabins, and knocked at all the doors. He called, but all was still. When he was satisfied that every person on board had been drowned he wept bitterly.

Friday stood there with open and staring eyes. He looked and looked. He was astonished at the large ship and at the wonderful things before him. They were in the cabin where the passengers had been. There stood trunks under the benches and clothes hung on the hooks on the wall. One trunk was open. In it were telescopes through which the travelers had looked at the land. Robinson saw also paper, pens, pen-holders and ink. Books were also near by. Robinson first took a thick book. It was the Bible, out of which his mother had so often taught him. Then they came to the sailors' cabin. There hung muskets and swords and bags of shot and cartridges. Then they went to the work-room. There were saws, hammers, spades, shovels, chisels, nails, bottles, and pails, knives and forks. And something more, over which Robinson was most glad, matches. At last they came into the store-room. There lay bags of flour and barley, teas, lentils, beans and sugar. Then Robinson embraced Friday in his great joy and said to him, "How rich we are!"

XXXIX

SAVING THINGS FROM THE SHIP

After Robinson had looked through the ship he began to plan the way to get the tools and things he most wanted on shore. He and Friday first carried everything together that he wanted to take on shore. When they had done this, he found he had the following things. Robinson stood everything together that he needed most.

1. A case of nails and screws.
2. Two iron axes and several hatchets.
3. A saw.
4. A small case of planes, tongs, augers, files, chisels, etc.
5. A third case with iron brackets, hooks, hinges, etc.
6. A case of matches.
7. A barrel of gunpowder.
8. Two muskets and a pistol.
9. Several swords.
10. A bag of cartridges.
11. A large sail cloth and some rope.
12. A telescope.

By means of the ship's ropes, Robinson let everything down into his boat. He himself took the Bible and then they rowed to the shore, and unloaded the boat. Everything was put into the bower where rain could not harm it. By the time they had this done, night was coming on and they decided to do no more that day, but wait until the next day.

"We must work fast," said Robinson. "The first storm is likely to break the ship in pieces and destroy everything in it."

The next morning early they ate a hastily prepared breakfast and were off to the boat. Neither Robinson nor Friday stopped for their noonday lunch. "A storm is brewing," said Robinson, "the air is calm, the sky is overcast with clouds, the heat is oppressive. We must hurry." With the utmost diligence they rowed back and forth all day. They made nine trips. They had now on shore a surprising quantity of all kinds of tools, goods and weapons. They had all kinds of ware to use in the kitchen, clothes, and food. Robinson prized a little four-wheeled wagon and a whetstone.

But in looking over his stores, Robinson suddenly discovered that he had no needles or thread. They went at once to procure these important articles. In looking for needles and thread, Robinson found a small trunk full of money and valuable stones. There were diamonds, rubies, pearls, and much gold. Robinson pushed it to one side. "What can I do with riches on this island? I would give them all for some needles and thread," he said to Friday. But on second thought he took the trunk and its contents along with him to his cave. For in the trunk were also letters and writings. "Perhaps," he said, "these tell to whom the valuables belong and I can return them some time."

Robinson at last found a case containing everything one could need with which to cut and sew cloth. There were scissors, thread, needles, thimbles, tapes, and buttons. But now the wind was rising and they must hurry. They were nearly ready for departure. They were passing through a part of the ship not before visited. They were surprised to hear a sound coming from a room whose door was kept shut by a heap of stuff that had been thrown against it by the violent pitching of the ship in the storm. Robinson and Friday cleared away the rubbish and were surprised to find a dog almost drowned. He was so weak from want of food that his cries could be heard a short distance only. Robinson took him tenderly in his arms and carried him to the boat, while Friday carried the sewing case and the trunk.

The wind was now blowing a gale. A few yards from the ship they were in great danger. Robinson grasped the rudder and made Friday stand ready to cut away the mast in case they found the wind too strong. With the greatest difficulty they finally made the little cove at the mouth of the creek and were soon landed with their precious cargo. The next morning they eagerly searched the waters for the ship. Not even their field glasses could reveal anything of it. Some planks, a mast, and parts of a small boat were blown on shore. All else had disappeared.

Robinson set to work at once to make a door for his bower out of the pine wood cast up by the waves. How easy the work proceeded with saws, hammers, augers, squares, planes, nails, hinges, and screws! With the wagon too, Friday could now gather his corn quickly and easily, or haul in a great quantity of grapes to dry for raisins.

Friday had never seen a gun. He did not know the use of firearms. The muskets that Robinson had brought from the ship were a great mystery to him. Robinson showed him their use. He showed how they could defend themselves. He told Friday that these weapons would kill at a distance. He took some powder and touched a match to it. Friday was greatly frightened.

Robinson then proceeded to load the gun. He put in some powder, a ball of lead or bullet. Then at the hammer he placed a little cap which gave a flash when struck. This ignited the powder. When all was in readiness Robinson bade Friday follow him. They went slowly out into the forest along the stream. Soon Robinson espied a rabbit sitting under a clump of grass. Robinson raised his gun, took careful aim, pressed the trigger. There was a flash and loud report and there lay the rabbit dead. But Friday, too, was lying on the ground. He had fainted from astonishment and fright. Robinson dropped his gun and raised the poor fellow up to a sitting position. He quickly recovered. He ran to get the rabbit. He examined it carefully. Robinson at last pointed out the hole the bullet had made and the mystery of the way the rabbit was killed was solved.

Robinson had lived alone so long that he had learned to love every living creature on the island. He never harmed anything except when he needed food. He had lived so quietly that the birds and animals did not fear him. They lived near his shelter and seemed to know him.

Robinson was delighted with his new tools and weapons. But they reminded him of home. Nothing that he had seen in all the time he had been on the island so turned his thoughts toward home and friends. Robinson would sit for hours thinking of the past and making plans for the future. He was homesick.

XL

THE RETURN OF THE SAVAGES

Robinson now renewed his plans for escaping from the island to Friday's country. They first rebuilt their boat with their new tools. They hollowed out the center till the sides were thin toward the top. They shaped her sides and keel. They made her prow sharp so that she would cut the water easily. They made a new mast, strong and tall and shapely. They made larger and stronger sails and ropes. They made two pairs of extra oars. They made boxes and cupboards in the prow and stern for keeping their fresh water and provisions. Friday's eyes sparkled with joy when it was done. He hoped he would now be able to return to his own island and parents. Robinson noticed his joy and asked him, "Do you want to return to your own people?"

"Yes," said Friday, "very much."

"Would you trust yourself in this boat?"

"Yes," said Friday.

"Very well," said his master, "you may have it and start home when you please.". "Yes, Master, but you come too, my people will not hurt you." Robinson resolved to venture over to Friday's land with him.

But before their preparations were complete the rainy season of our fall set in. They resolved to wait until the weather was settled and as soon as the rainy season was over to set out. They ran their boat well up into the creek and covered it over with a large tarpaulin made of sail-cloth obtained from the ship.

Robinson had now been on the island twenty-seven years. For the last three years he had lived happily with his companion Friday. Every year in September, Robinson celebrated the day his life was saved and he was thrown up on the island. Robinson celebrated it this year with more than the usual thankfulness. He thought that it would be his last anniversary on the island.

One morning, Friday had gone to the beach to find a turtle. Soon he came running back out of breath. "O Master," he cried, "they are coming, they are coming to take me prisoner!" He was trembling with fright.

"We must take our guns and defend ourselves," said Robinson. "But we will not kill anyone unless they attack us." This quieted Friday. They loaded four muskets and three pistols. Robinson put the pistols in his belt, where he also fastened a sword. He gave Friday a pistol and a musket, for Friday had learned to shoot well. Besides Friday carried a bag of powder and bullets. Robinson took his field glasses and saw twenty-one savages with two prisoners. The prisoners were bound and lying on the ground. This was a war party celebrating a victory with a feast. They probably intended to kill their prisoners. "We must save the lives of those men," said Robinson.

The savages this time had landed quite near Robinson's shelter, not more than a half mile below the creek's mouth. Soon he and Friday started off. Robinson commanded Friday to follow quietly and not to speak or shoot.

"We will surprise them and give them a good scare," said Robinson.

When yet a considerable distance away they could hear the savages yelling and screaming. Some of them were dancing their war dance. Their faces and bodies were painted to make them look terrible to their enemies. They were dancing around their prisoners with hideous cries and gestures. They could now see the prisoners plainly. One had a beard and was plainly a white man. Robinson was surprised and determined to save him at all risks.

"Get your gun ready to fire," he said to Friday, "and when I say the word let us run forward yelling and firing our guns over their heads. This will fill them with such fright that they will take to their heels and boats and get away as soon as possible. In the scramble and confusion we will rush in and rescue the prisoners."

This plan did not please Friday at all. His savage blood was up and he wanted to kill all he could. "Let's fire on them," he said. "Let's kill all but the prisoners."

"No, no," said Robinson, "it's always wrong to take life unless it cannot be avoided to save one's own. Let's try my plan first."

With great reluctance Friday consented. At a signal from Robinson they rushed forward, and when in plain sight they fired off their muskets in the air. If the ground had suddenly exploded beneath their feet there could have been no more confusion, astonishment, and fright. A few took to their heels. Others lay as if dead. They had swooned from fright. But as Robinson came up they jumped to their feet and pushed into the boats, leaving the prisoners behind. Robinson and Friday still rushed forward and fired their remaining loaded guns and pistols in the air. The savages made all haste to get into their boats and push off. Soon they were well out to sea, paddling rapidly for the west. Robinson reloaded his arms and gave them a farewell volley, but not a soul was killed or even wounded. This gave Robinson great pleasure. He had accomplished his purpose without bloodshed.

They could now turn to the prisoners. Robinson ran back to them and quickly cut their ropes. Robinson asked the white man who he was, but the man was too weak to answer. Robinson gave him a piece of bread.

The fear of death being removed, the white man soon grew stronger. When Friday came running back from watching the boats and saw the savage that had been a prisoner he gave a loud yell. He threw his arms around the man, kissed him and laughed and cried for joy. He put his head on his breast and hugged him again and again. Robinson was greatly surprised and puzzled. He asked Friday what his actions meant. But so intent was Friday that he got no answer.

At last Friday recovered far enough from his great joy to say with face beaming with delight, "O, Master, this man is my dear father." They at once began a long conversation, each one told his story. Suddenly Friday jumped up and said, "How foolish I am, I have not thought to give my father anything to eat and drink. He must be nearly starved." And away he ran toward the shelter and was soon back with food and water to drink.

Robinson learned through Friday from his father that the white man was a Spaniard, that he had been captured by the tribe that had a battle with Friday's people. The Spaniard was one of sixteen men that had been saved by Friday's people from a wrecked ship. So weak were the prisoners that they could not walk to the shelter. Robinson and Friday made a litter and carried them one after the other. When once there, Friday prepared some rich rice soup. The prisoners ate heartily and in a few days were strong enough to go about the island.

XLI

DELIVERANCE AT LAST

Friday had not forgotten the plan for going to his home. He would often mention it and spent hours talking about it during the long rainy season. But now that the Spaniard and Friday's father had come into the family, Robinson felt he must change his plans a little. He felt very sorry for the Spaniards left in Friday's country. They did not have enough to eat and were sick and sad besides. He talked the matter over with the Spaniard many times. They at last planned to send for them. The Spaniard and Friday's father were to go. Robinson was for doing it at once. But the Spaniard advised delay. "How can we get food for ourselves and fifteen others? Your small store will soon be used up," he argued. Robinson at last saw that this difficulty must be overcome. There was just one thing to do, and this, to delay their departure until a new crop of corn could be raised. This would take six months.

But at it they went. The four men could do much and work fast. They cleared more ground and planted all the seed corn they could spare from their store. Besides this they sowed about twelve bushels of barley they had gotten in the ship.

The care for so much crop, its harvesting and storing away, kept them very busy for the season. Robinson not only did this, but also increased his flock of goats by catching kids and putting them in his pasture. He gathered, too, all the grapes he could and dried them on the branches of trees.

At the end of the harvesting season, they made ready their boat. They filled it with all the bread it could well carry. They put in raisins and fresh water. Robinson gave the Spaniard and Friday's father each a musket and plenty of powder and bullets. Now, all was ready. Friday gave his father a loving farewell. He stretched out his arms towards him as the boat moved away. The Spaniard and Robinson waved their hats and they were off.

They promised to be back in eight or nine days. Robinson and Friday made every preparation to receive the guests. They were to have a home not far from Robinson's built of poles, and thatched with the long marsh grasses, like Robinson's bower. There was no need of hiding or defending it. It did not take long to fix it up.

Eight days had now passed since the boat had left. Friday could hardly restrain himself longer. He watched the ocean all the time. He would go to the top of the hill with the field glasses every hour during the day to catch a first glimpse of them.

On the ninth day, as Friday put up his glasses to search the waters he dropped them with a yell of surprise. He tore down the hill with the utmost speed and rushed up to Robinson as one gone mad. "Look, look, O Master!" he cried, "a big ship; a big ship way out on the sea!" Robinson took the glasses, and sure enough, there within hailing distance was a large ocean going vessel. Robinson was overcome with excitement.

For twenty-eight years his aching eyes had scanned the waters for this welcome sight. His joy was boundless. The ship looked like an American. Yes, there floated the American flag! How welcome a sight to Robinson. He could not utter a word. Tears filled his eyes and streamed down his cheeks. He would soon have news from home. He ran to the shore and shot off a gun to attract the attention of those on board. He heard answering shots at once.

Soon a boat was lowered and in it three men rowed toward the shore. It was the captain himself and two sailors. The captain was astonished to find a man in the lonely island. Robinson told how it all had happened and how he would like to return home. To his unspeakable delight the captain told him that the ship was bound for New York and would take him along free of charge, but he must leave that day. The ship could not be delayed any longer. Of course Robinson would go. Friday was beside himself with grief. He did not want to be left behind alone. He did not know that the Spaniards would ever return. Something might happen to them on the sea. But before the eventful day the Spaniards landed. They brought word that Friday's father had died after his return home. Friday was thrown into a fit of grief at the news. He wept and repeated over and over his praise of the good man.

XLII

ROBINSON AT HOME

It was with a sad heart that Robinson made ready to leave. Every familiar place seemed now doubly dear to him. He went from one to another with tears in his eyes. Here lay his home. Here were his fields, his crops and his goats. Everything was the work of his own hands. He had made them all. Which should he take? He hesitated long. He must take home some of his belongings to show the people at home. And there were his parrot and the dog which had won a place in Robinson's heart. He decided to take them along. At length he got together his diary, his parasol, his Bible, his treasures, a suit of clothes, his dog, and a hat. He had saved, too, his bow and arrows. These he decided to take along. Everything else he gave to his good man Friday and the Spaniard who wished to be allowed to remain on the island.

Robinson kissed Friday tenderly. He with great effort finally tore himself away and ran to the shore where the ship's boat awaited him. But Robinson had not counted on the strength of Friday's love for him. Robinson's boat had not yet reached the ship when Friday sprang into the water and swam after him shouting, "Master, take me with you, I would rather die than stay here without you." Robinson was touched at the devotion showed by the faithful Friday, and gave orders to turn the boat back, and take him on board. The anchor was raised. The ship started on her way to the home Robinson had left so long ago.

The wind was favorable and in seven weeks the spires and buildings of his native city were in sight. His vessel came slowly up to the wharf where he had taken ship so many years ago. Here, too, he had played and idled his time away. He remembered it all. His idleness and playing truant came back in sad memories. Before Robinson and Friday landed, their good friend the captain gave them each a new suit of clothes.

Everything had changed. He scarcely knew the place. He was astonished and confused by the din, hurry and bustle of a great city. Friday seemed dazed by it all and clung to Robinson's side. The buildings were so tall, the street cars, the carriages were different.

Everywhere there were iron machines, casting out smoke, puffing and running about on iron rails. Robinson had never seen these.

Robinson, however, did not stop to admire; he pushed on to a certain street and house where lived his parents at the time of his departure. It was with difficulty that he found the place. It was now in the heart of the city. Upon inquiry he found, after much searching, that his father had removed his store and home to another part of the city, his mother had died of grief for her disobedient son. Robinson was sorely grieved at this. He had hoped to see her and tell her how sorry he was that he had caused her so much anxiety and sorrow.

When he had found the place where his father lived he stole quietly up to the house and opened the door. His father, now a gray-haired man, bent with age and sorrow, was sitting in his armchair reading.

Robinson came forward, but his father did not recognize him. "Who are you?" he said. "I am Robinson, your long-lost son." He knelt by his father's side and asked forgiveness for all the trouble he had caused. His father was overcome. He could not speak. He drew Robinson with feeble hands to his breast. "My son, I forgive you," he said.

Robinson's boyhood friends heard of his strange return. They had thought him dead long ago. They never tired of hearing him tell his strange story. They pitied him in his misfortune. But Robinson told them that it all happened to him because he was idle and disobedient in his youth.

Robinson at once relieved his father at the store. The business thrived. His father died. He soon had a home of his own with a happy family. Friday, the dog, and the parrot lived in it, dearly beloved and cared for by their master the rest of their days. In the home there is a young Robinson who loves to hear his father read from his diary of the wonderful things that happened on the island.

Robinson tried many times to find the rightful owner of the gold and jewels, but never succeeded. At last he gave them to a school where boys with idle habits were taught to lead useful and industrious lives